12 Harrows Close

A Dearth of Magic
Book 3

Matthew Wennersten

Published by

Heroes of Modern Legend

USA | India | New Zealand | Worldwide

ISBN: 978-0-9975741-4-2

Cover design by Sathya Ganapathi

Cover photos Ehimetalor Akhere Unuabona *and* Bruno Martins *on* Unsplash

For Ashwati and Andrea, and the rest of the black sheep out there

CONTENTS

UNDERWATER

Vic gets fit, and a little hot under the collar

Nearly two years on from the pandemic, public health emergency, however you described it, everything was still jangled, not quite back to normal. Vic knew she was lucky, considering. For her, it had been a decent pandemic. Or not decent. Hard to call millions of people dying of respiratory failure decent.

Like everyone else in England, when the virus hit Italy, she hadn't taken it too seriously. Pubs stayed full. It only affected old people. A few weeks later, everyone was sick. And then really sick. Or they knew someone who was. Followed by the chaos of the government response, as if brain cells were too occupied with political manoeuvres to care for basic health. Once the initial confusion, fear, and anger had numbed, she had learned a few things. Amidst the anxiety, Vic found she didn't need company as much as she'd thought. Certainly not as much as she used to.

Her work had helped her through, that and the diving. It had taken some mental and physical adjustments. The mental surprised her more. She'd thought at first both would be more body than mind. Steady hands. Strong lungs. Especially since she had never been much of a swimmer.

Before the lockdown, she'd been taking lessons again at the Leisure Centre. It was her, a middle-aged Asian, and a flock of toddlers, all cheerful splashes and churning legs crowned with bright-coloured water wings. She made good progress once she told off the coach for being insincere. No need for 'good job', ta very much, she had purpose in mind. If a four-year-old could keep his head in the water, she could as well. Then scuba lessons. It was pure luck she'd squeezed in enough hours to certify before they closed the pools.

Another discovery: once you'd mastered the fear, swimming underwater could be effortless. The real trick was to conserve energy, keep the breathing light, align with the feel of the water. Let the natural movement of the currents help you where you want to go. Find a new layer when the currents turned. After a year, she would burn through the battery of her underwater torch faster than the oxygen cylinder. She'd drift across the bottom of the Thames, sipping slowly at the big tank, heart rate steady as the occasional, always remarkable, fish observed her back. She'd been particularly proud of her reaction when the oversized boot of her diving costume held fast in the muck. Snared by a broken skein of fishing line, she'd checked her oxygen gauge. How long do I have before I slice off my foot, she'd thought.

The work was equally unexpected. As cases mounted and health officials on the telly talked of lockdowns, she had supposed it was the end for the furniture workshop. Most of what Vic thought of as the "gold brick money" had gone right back into the house. Her father might have kept a survivalist-getaway-plan gold bar in the basement for when the house became uninhabitable. Vic wanted to actually inhabit the house. To be fair, grab your 'go bag' and escape into the night was tempting when she found out the cost of double glazing. How did it get so expensive? Would have been cheaper to replace all the windows with Macbooks.

The rest of what was left from the gold bar, she sank into the business. Perhaps a larger portion than was truly necessary went into bulk orders of delicious tropical hardwoods. There was something about mahogany and rosewood that sent her beyond rational budgeting. Certainly, beyond the price the market would bear. The over-ambitious rare wood inventory did give her enough buffer to get kicked around a few times on unpaid commissions and not go under. She tried not to dwell on the clients who demanded back the deposit after they'd seen pictures of work in construction. What were they thinking? That there was a line of people wanting these very same bespoke cabinets, to fit the exact 27.5 cm gap in their coincidentally matching teak panels?   But scathing Etsy reviews were bad for business. You smiled over the phone and hoped for a 26-ish cm order that you could plane down and make fit.

Four months into the lockdown, she'd twigged to it. Selling Brazilian hardwoods at cost to doom-scrollers was a losing game. Especially when they delayed payment until the refund for their cancelled Marbella trip came through. Good luck collecting on that. The same hardwood could be sold at ten times the price to a different set. A set equally frightened and caged at home, but in bigger homes, with more room for fancy furniture. Exceptionally fancy. The kind of folk for whom, "Are you sure you can afford it?" was inconceivably vulgar.

Those types were more concerned with exclusivity. Young up-and-coming artist, made by hand, can only make a few sticks a year. Your piece made uniquely for you. Check. Or rather, cheque and ka-ching. Victoria Ali Bespoke went strictly upscale. The odd thing was that whether priced at cost or ten times, she sold the same amount of furniture – slightly more than she could reasonably manufacture on her own. At ten times cost, she could afford to take on Rahim. So she did. As the nightly news talked up record sales at off-licenses, her order book filled with liquor sideboards. Tasteful and office-appropriate when caught on the Zoom camera, natch.

Nowhere to go, furniture sales up, she had spent most of the lockdown hunched over power-tools or driving to London to dive. Spike Island was quarantined to the public but open all hours to anyone with the energy to create through the malaise. During the day, she'd swim. Dusk, she'd drive on empty highways back to Rahim at the studio.

Rahim managed the e-commerce, helped on deliveries, and did the dailies on the accounts. Usually, they'd go over spreadsheets and statements together, then Rahim would show her what setups he'd done in the studio. This often ended in a lesson from Vic – the best way to counter-sink wood screws, the right mix for the epoxy to doubly secure the joins. Rahim had cleverly setup a separate online store for more mass market items. Called it Modern Legends. After a year, Rahim was making much of the Legends catalogue on his own. Vic would do quality checks and the occasional fix, then work deep into the night, alone.

At least once a fortnight, she or Rahim would finish a substantial piece. 350ml Cava for her, fizzy apple from the mini-fridge in the studio corner for him, they celebrated progress by the circles of missing cans imprinted in the cardboard bottom of the Tesco's cases.

Steady work, regular exercise, training Rahim, settling into her father's house. It helped the days pass, despite the constant background terror. Between the diving and the manual labour, she was more fit than she could remember. Which is not to say she couldn't relate when others described their struggle with feelings of impending doom. Still, she knew she'd have been more afraid of the virus if it were the only dread visitor likely to come calling.

For all the weight of expectation, when the necklace warmed, it was terrifying. Dan had cautioned her to never take it off. She hadn't, home, sleeping in it despite the weight of the gold coins. She'd had a sudden, physical flash on the one time she'd been sunburned, out all day in a low-cut swimming costume. The water had been a cruel tease from the heat. It was too cold to manage more than a brief dip and run out, yelping and hyperventilating, sun too hot to lay out in. Black girls don't burn, right? Vic still remembered how she'd had to shower in cold water, chest too sensitive for the hot water tap. The next day was itchy, followed by an ashy peel. Must have been the hole in the ozone layer.

It felt like that, the heat on her chest that woke her.

She lay in bed, listening, the hottest point moving slowly along the chain of the necklace, as if tracking something circling the house outside. She heard the occasional noise as it shifted position, light footsteps she would probably not have identified without the hot radar encircling her neck. She ran through scenarios in her mind, processing in parallel with the animal response that soaked the sheets with sour sweat. It moved away without explanation, faint sounds fading into a silence Vic felt as a cooling on her chest.

It forced her to admit she had been unprepared for an event long expected, which rankled. Time to join the gun club. Although Vic found that she liked shooting. Ever-practical, Fatima had long encouraged her to do something to protect herself. Which didn't stop her from chucking a wobbly when Vic told her she was applying for a gun license. But what good was a taser, or tae kwan do, against the kind of beast that was hunting her?

Her first attempt at a shotgun license foundered on the 'binding over' order from the motorcycle excursion into the Thames. It seemed that the recognizance under which she had been released did not include firearms. But the public health emergency fixed that. Idly wandering the web during lockdown, an online form helpfully informed her that her period of restriction, as it was put, ended in November. Would she like to upload a passport photograph and reference letter? Rahim helped her craft the under-bed gun safe, although supply chain tangles meant she'd had to wait three weeks for the biometric reader to squeeze through the Suez Canal. Three weeks waiting with a shotgun wrapped only in Mal's old carpet under the bed.

Her father had had no opinion on guns. Of course, he knew they were dangerous. Certainly, it wasn't what any one of her friends would have done. There were other, more martial families – a son expected to carry on the tradition, a bright photo with an Army beret matching the more muted black-and-white shots of great uncles and obscure cousins, the ones who had fought in the wars. Or not wars anymore, she thought. Conflicts. There was a boy at school everyone knew would enlist. Plus another one who surprised them, appearing one day at the pub the year after failing his A-levels. He was leaner, taller than they remembered, a digital patterned jacket with his name stenciled on it. She heard he'd had his hand blown off in Iraq helping the Americans. Vague rumours he'd become a gardener, with help from Royal Army disability.

It was somehow known that her family, her friends' families, no matter how on the edge they might be, would be doctors, engineers, writers, scientists. Not soldiers. The fashion designers in waiting were obvious, as were the free spirits who might not make it back from teaching English in Korea, or backpacking across Ecuador. The waiters-cum-thespians, no one from her school shiny enough to be a likely movie star. For them, a shotgun was as likely as a laser beam. Or as likely as Vic becoming a lorry driver. Yet there she was, driving a delivery van with a bumper decal for the Cwmbran Rifle and Shotgun Association.

Lord knew whether a shotgun would actually help, should that thing return. Didn't matter – the gun safe gave her a measure of comfort. Roll onto the floor, finger on the glass reader, out pops the 12-gauge Browning over-under. Not going out had given her plenty of time to do research. Handy during the Zoom interview for her 'sporting license'. She was almost jolly in debating the merits of Hollands versus Remingtons. Approved by the constable who tried to convince her birdshot would bounce off well-oiled goose feathers at range. Unlikely. She loaded 00 buckshot in any event. But would even that do any good?

GREAT EXPECTATIONS

Fatima plans for retirement, Moscow auditions to be the new Rome

Vic unzipped the front of her suit and hauled her empty oxygen cylinder back to the van. In theory, she could have kept her phone with her, but coverage underwater was chancy, and what would she do if it buzzed? Neoprene wing flapping, she fished her phone from beneath the driver's seat. Vic's useful but highly annoying super-power was an uncanny sense for the missed call. Fatima. With voicemail. Who uses voicemail? Could be big news, or perhaps Fatima had failed to hit the hang-up button.

It reminded Vic of, what would you call it? Her night visitor? Ghoulish stalker? Whatever. After it came and went, she'd called Fatima. That was the last time she'd left a voicemail. A terrified voicemail, followed by two hours clenched tight on the couch before Fats called her back. The conversation was etched in memory, Fatima at her most typically pitiless. "What did you think would happen?"

"I don't know."

"Well, your strategy is succeeding brilliantly."

"What strategy?"

"Waiting to be killed."

"Damn it, Fatima, do you have a better idea?"

"Yes, in fact, I do. I gave them to you last year, before this stupid pandemic."

"Right, travel the world with Dan. As if he'd want my company. Or me his."

"That was one. Get very very lost was another. Alaska. Okinawa. New Zealand."

"Yes," replied Vic, "and your third brilliant idea was to live in a commune with lots of people around–"

"Kibbutz," Fatima interrupted, "but yes, that was the general idea. Kibbutz in particular, despite, or, correction, because of their politics. Israeli guns are real and marksmanship training well distributed."

"As if guns were the answer. We don't even know if they'll feel a bullet."

"Normally a fair point, but we don't have evidence against, and no better alternative springs to mind. I'm worried about you, Vix. I don't have so many friends that I can afford to let one, oh, I don't know, unleash a plague of undead soul-eating monsters on the world because she was too proud to take elementary precautions?"

Only Fatima could have managed a phrase like that without stopping for breath.

"So, what, guns?"

"Well, hopefully not. But active measures."

"Active?"

"Yes, active. God, Vic, I hate having to talk to you like you're an idiot. Tell the police you're being stalked. Call Dan. Start digging around. What else have you found in your coal mine of a house?"

Vic uncurled from the blanket. Her left foot had gone to sleep. So much for vigilance. "Not much. Stale military surplus and a bad feeling. One gold bar."

"No books, no notes, no hidden passages?" asked Fatima, a bit gentler.

"I wish. I think Dad had moved all his notes to soft copy. His main laptop was stolen."

"What about cloud backups?"

"I asked your husband to have a butchers. So far, no luck."

"Did you call Dan?"

"Phoned and emailed. He's off the grid."

A new ping snapped the chain of memory. What was that ad campaign? Keep situational awareness? Which would be the opposite of chewing on an old conversation when you need to be awake in the present. Text message from Fatima. 'Did you get the voicemail', no question mark. Vic put the phone on the van seat to manoeuvre her arms out of the bulky suit. This call would need some gesturing. She touched the icon to call Fatima.

Pickup was instantaneous. "Where were you? I've called, messaged, big news."

"Blowing bubbles."

"Oh, what? Diving? Right-o. Well, guess what?"

"You've been made editor of The Sun," replied Vic.

"No, you git." Vic felt the foot stamp through the phone. "Guess again."

"George's mum is minor royalty, and you're distantly in line to the throne."

"Way off, Vixen. I'm pregnant!"

"You?"

"I KNOW. Isn't it exciting?"

"That's one word for it."

"Oh, stop it. George is super excited. And super nervous. I'm a combination of all that, plus impatient. New life out of the pandemic."

"And eighteen years of responsibility," added Vic.

"Ha. I figure about twelve. Zero to one is me. During infancy, Dot should be able to take care...."

"I'm sorry, who?"

"Dot. Dorothy. My mother-in-law. George's mum." Fatima continued. "Early sixties, in decent nick. I'll get the sprog weaned and take off for breaks as needed. By the time they're eight, school is most of the day, eight-year-olds can dress and feed themselves, really, it's only until about sixteen you have to do anything. By then, they're sullen and overproud to take advice from parents anyway. Besides, sixteen and a half years from now, George should be getting ready to retire. Put the offspring in uni and revisit the world."

Vic rolled her eyes. "Somehow, I suspect this child adventure won't go according to plan. Remember your childhood?"

"I do. Mostly benign neglect. Except for the schoolwork, which I took care of anyway. Time to bring back the old 'seen but not heard', I say. Not sure what happened to people our age. Have you seen the parenting blogs? It's a new world. I must say I find the competitive aspect a bit strange. Lessons for this, summer programs for that, make sure they're speaking Mandarin by age three, as if China was going to take over the world. But what do you really think, Vic?"

Vic sighed, then gathered herself. "Happy for you? I think I'm happy for you. Honestly. Boy or girl?"

"Dunno, it's still first trimester. Kind of enjoying the not knowing. George, typical, has gone into full planner mode. Spreadsheets and catalogues. I've ruled out light blue and pink, regardless of gender, assigned or otherwise."

"I'll make you a cradle."

"You'll do more than that. I'm expecting frequent visitations, post-partum cheer-ups, complete acquiescence on babysitting when needed. And no disapproving looks at the occasional wine glass. I get enough of that from George. Now, what's been happening? Any return visits from your... "

"Night visitor? Neighborhood ghoul? I was literally just thinking about it. Thankfully, no. Nothing. It's been months. Strangest thing, one night of insane terror, a complete circumnavigation of the house, then, gone. It's like they were staking out the place, doing a recce–"

"Or perhaps a boundary?" interrupted Fatima. "Some ward or protection your father put in place?"

"Hardly," replied Vic. "We talked about this, remember? If there was anything, it would have gone off when Dad was attacked, or it would have stopped the attack in the first place. I expect I'm no safer there than anywhere else. Probably less safe. Easy to find."

"Unless there's another ward or weapon hidden somewhere. You still haven't done a full accounting of what's in your cellar."

Vic shrugged off the shoulder strap of her dry suit trousers before answering. "Fats, I'm not sure why you go on about this. It's possible there's a secret passage. Or a well-hidden box we've yet to find. But unlikely. We've given it a good going over. There's nothing down there now except a few boxes of Mal's old junk."

"Which you should throw out or give away, you know."

Vic felt the heat rise in her face. "No, Fatima. I don't know. Or rather, I know it's doubtful he's coming back. But I'm not ready to write him off. I've been diving now for a year and a half, and I'm getting pretty good at it. Which is to say that I'm learning the Thames currents. Chances of finding him in that murky mess are snowballs. Even less likely than finding a magical bangle in the basement. But that doesn't mean I am going to do one thing about his boxes."

"Oh, Vic." Vic could picture Fatima in the flat in London, probably wearing one of George's old concert tees. "I'm never going to tell you how to run your life. Heaven knows I've made some odd choices. My parents still aren't thrilled about George, even. But have you thought about dating?" asked Fatima. "They have apps for that, you know. Bumble. Hinge."

"I know. Tinder."

"Eww. Nobody uses Tinder anymore, except for sex."

"A bit of sex I wouldn't mind."

"Right then. Take them into the woods in your cute little van."

Vic looked at the van in question. Metallic blue, a bit

boxy, big enough for a mattress in the back if you don't mind driving with a bungee cord to hold the rear door shut. She and Rahim had delivered a loveseat and coffee table yesterday, which meant there was nothing in back today but the oxygen tanks strapped to the mesh bulkhead behind her seat. "Soon, Fats, soon. I'm not convinced people are who they are at the moment."

"You mean, from the pandemic?"

"Yes, that. Hard to be your free and natural self with a bit of constant low-grade anxiety and depression. But also, it's our time of life. You know I prefer them a little older."

"As in centuries older," replied Fatima.

"I'll ignore that. But the guys in the late thirties and early forties? If they've never been married, they're too into themselves. And too fast. The formerly married ones are creepy. Or bitter. Learned all the wrong lessons from their divorces. And also too into themselves. Sooo much work. I'd rather have a glass of prosecco with you. Which we're still doing, pregnant or not."

"That's the spirit. Let's do it soon, eh? I'm still worried you'll get eaten by some creature in the night."

"Yeah," said Vic. "Me too." She gave the side of her van an absentminded pat. "I'm shooting again this weekend if you want to come. There's a twee pub not too far from the range. Bring George."

"We're going to Birmingham Sunday, to break the news to Dot in person."

"Come Saturday and stay the night. It's quicker to Birmingham from Bristol anyway."

"We just might, Vics," said Fatima, in the kind way friends say no. "Let me talk to the hubby. I'll message you. Ta."

Vic unslung the other strap of her suit trousers and stamped her now-familiar way through the fumbling dance required to get the heavy fabric off. So easy in the water, so clumsy on land. She shook the suit a few times to get the last drops off, then threw it into the back. It lay like a dead body on the yoga mats she'd hot-glued to the metal floor of the van. Shavasana. Not enough roofline to do standing poses. But the mats did keep the deliveries from sliding around.

Good thing the boat club had an outdoor shower. For the 'bathers'. It was perfect to stand under in the dry suit and sluice off debris from the river. She loved the sensation of being marvelously dry within a downpour. Not sure who in their right mind might wish to bathe in the Thames in winter. Or any time of year, given the muck. But they did.

Vic had struck up a talking acquaintanceship with a few of the swimmers last summer. Outdoor sports, socially distant, mostly triathletes or ultra-long-distance swimmers. A variety of ages and genders, but remarkably uniform in appearance. Deeply tanned, ropy veins over striated muscles, flat stomachs, broad chests. A little more long-limbed, a bit thinner in the face than average. Conversations never moved much past the initial 'hallo' and 'fancy sunglasses'. She had bonded with a few over the meditative aspect of being in the water, but diving didn't move you in the same way. The pace was different. The ultras sought to lose themselves in the effort of pushing against. Vic sought something else. What that was, she realised, she was no longer sure.

– § –

Two in the morning in Moscow, the lobby of the Hotel Barin Grand Residence was buzzy. It had been the same throughout the pandemic, women in heels and matching cheekbones, coats below hemlines, red flashing soles reflecting in the tan marble floor, escorted by men well past their rendezvous with dumpy middle-age. A comfortable age, judging by the Ferraris and Lamborghinis they arrived in, assuming the price of Bitcoin held up.

A colorless figure sat alone in the atrium café, leafing through the pages of a burgundy folio. A Russian passport, with his face on the identity page. Roman.

Roman Baranski. At least it started with R, he thought. He nudged the grey sports bag further under the table with his foot. What are names, anyway? Roman, Reggie, Rex, Roger, Remy. Some more brief than others. His parents had named him René. He no longer spoke French in public. The accent gave him away, someone 'not from here' no matter where here was. The distance between the words of his youth and today's slang farther than geography. He had no ear for it. Despite that, he had lived in England long enough to pick up a rough, vague, could be from the Midlands English. His Russian was terrible. Enough to satisfy an immigration officer or order a meal from the local menu. When pressed, he pointed to his ears and the dent in his forehead, with vague 'don't understand' gestures.

People understood that he'd been in an accident. Except it had not been an accident. When the stake in his heart hadn't killed him, they had tried to put one through his head. Too bad for them the helper had taken his hand off the rope to hold the second stake. With the rope binding his hands loose, it was easy. The foolhardy helper died first, of a light touch to the bare skin of the wrist holding the spike. Then a wrestling match for the spike itself. Roman put the stake into the eye of the hammer wielder while the three remaining rope helpers watched, wild with uncertainty. Do they let go and risk turning to dust? Or simply run? There was no place to run. They had barred the door to keep him from escaping.

Two died in the room. The third leapt from the window in a shatter of watery glass. Window fragments made a thin halo around the awkward crumple of his body below. Roman remembered thinking at the time, if two had jumped, one might have survived. He was grateful for their indecision. Healing the hole in his chest had taken most of what he had 'borrowed'. The mark in his forehead he left as a reminder. He had been Richard then, incautious, and indiscreet. Richard fled to England that night. Made friends. Not exactly.

Roman flicked through the passport pages again. New-ish, with a few stamps. The Netherlands. Germany. Austria. Probably a replacement, not a forgery, the face and digital fingerprint of the real Baranski swapped with his own. Zeroes and ones, they had said, smart Russian hackers with American TV-accented English. T-shirts under expensive slept-in suits. Shoes shined by the old men at the stalls in the metro. After the zeroes and ones, Arkady told him that his 'special talents' were insufficient to make him worth keeping around.

"We have enough ways to make people disappear. And mostly, we don't need to. Our targets are overseas, on the Internet. Either they pay, or they don't. No violence, no threat to us. The only people organising killings here are the government. The same government that protects us, for a small fee. So, thank you, but no."

"And who will protect you from me?" he had asked.

Arkady had shaken his head, a teacher with an exasperating student. "That is why we have helped you. And we will continue to help you. Evgeny will leave a passport for you with the concierge. That's the best we can do."

"I was promised money."

Arkady had only shrugged, the gesture unrumpling his suit coat slightly. "That part of the deal didn't go through. People are looking for you. People to whom it is difficult to say no. We've kept you out of sight, kept you safe. Perhaps you can take your talents to South Beach."

He was still Reggie then. "Are you mocking me?"

"No, tovarisch," said Arkady, in a quiet voice. "It's time to go, that's all. Zhenya will have the passport ready tonight." His companion had nodded. The hacker had spread his arms, helpless. They left in a cold puff of early evening Moscow air.

Roman tucked the passport away in his own suit jacket. Less crumpled, if less expensive than those of his erstwhile friends. He had changed his look since coming to Moscow. Trying to blend in. Pale features an asset in

Russia, one of the few he had, less money behind him than the software kids. He could stretch to a plane ticket, and not much more. No to first class, or checked baggage. He looked at the carry-on at his feet. No matter. He had always traveled light. He took an older model Android phone from another pocket and searched for a contact.

"Da?"

"Arkady? Roman."

"Ah, good, you got the passport."

"Yes. One more favor, and I'll fly out tonight. A small one."

"I'm listening. But be careful. Others may be too."

JUST DESSERTS

News comes through many channels, George cooks something up

Rahim's ringtone was a download of Jorja Smith's 'Be Honest'. Ms. Vic had put him on to it. He liked the music, but also found it amusing for his phone to call out, "You want this." His mum, not so much. Another reason why it was time to move out, to his own place. Ms. Vic said that if things kept this busy through the rest of the season, she'd be able to give him a raise. Which made Rahim one of the few people rooting for more lockdown, seeing as he and Vic did home furniture, and people going out didn't spend as much on the nesting. And that was the phone. The boss-lady. "Hello?"

"Rahim!" After a year and a bit, he still enjoyed the sound of Victoria's voice. "I'll be in shortly. Anything we need, or can I come straight to the studio?"

"One enquiry, Ms. Vic, but you'll have to call them to confirm the materials. We do need more acetone, if you're stopping by the home centre."

"Sod it, Rahim, we'll do that on the weekend. I've still

got at least six hours to go before we finish the...what is that thing?"

"Gun and fishing rod case. Extra tall, with narrower brackets on one side."

"Hmm," replied Vic. "We need to be charging more for that. I'm not keen."

"We could charge more if we spent more in online ads and hired someone to help make them. We've built up a bit of a brand. 'Emir Cabinetry by Modern Legends.'"

"I know." Vic laughed. "'King of Outdoors.' You staying late tonight?" she asked. "I can pick us up something on the way."

Rahim listened to the soft swish of the van's windscreen wipers while he thought it over. She was already in motion. "No thank you. I should get home before the rains become very heavy. Tonight's forecast may convince the Tories of climate change. Be prepared to sleep at the studio if you do come in. One second." Rahim scanned the scribbled notes on the desk they'd made from a kitchen cabinet gone wrong. "There is one more thing. An encrypted email."

"What's in it?"

"Ms. Vic, it's encrypted. I can't read it. You open it and it asks for an OTP. I didn't click it, as I thought it would go to your phone."

"Right. Paying more attention to the road than to you.

Sorry. I'll check it when I get in. Stay safe, Rahim."

Finding a park near the studio was an unwelcome chore. Working nights as she did, Vic often parked with a bit of cheek in the loading bay. She'd put the studio placard behind the windscreen. She'd only been called out a few times. Good thing she always had something heavy to bring down to the van as an excuse. Amazing how the gents (and it was almost always gents) would melt when they saw a lady lugging furniture. 'I didn't realize you were having trouble', or, 'Let me give you a hand with that'. Vic often wondered what would happen if, after the long look at her figure, she had dropped her facemask to reveal broken teeth. Or an acid scar. And no longer so young. The grey was starting to give that game away, that awkward middle ground between 'fit bird' and 'old woman'. Soon she'd reach the uncanny valley of 'might be work'. Which was fine – she was worth a bit of work. They'd finish helping her, no doubt. But would they so consistently store the studio number, 'in case she needed help again?'

This evening, someone had beaten her to it. Unfortunately legitimate – a flatbed lorry with an electric pallet lift. The lift operator was loading something rectangular and shrink-wrapped. Looked like an oversize canvas from one of the other studios.

I don't know how George does it, thought Vic. His panel van was huge. Much bigger than her little Nissan e-NV. He consistently managed to stroll in within minutes of his 'almost there' text. Must have some kind of sixth sense for spots. There was usually a park under the motorway ramp to the island, but with all the artists and vegans around here, the charging station there was rarely unoccupied. Besides, it was a ten-minute walk along cold rail tracks, and wet. While it was fun to catch up on the latest graffiti, the loading bay was better.

In truth, Vic admitted, tonight wasn't that bad. She found a spot only three blocks away and hauled up on the parking brake. She had gotten into a bit of a row with the salesman when she bought the EV. Automatic transmissions have a Park setting, so why also set the emergency brake? By the third lecture, this time from Rahim, she gave up. A year and a half of pandemic deliveries, often with heavy loads, had made it a habit. She sighed. Getting sensible, Vicky. At least she didn't have to wear sensible clothes. She threw her red leather jacket over the fleece top. It clashed with the purple fleece, but who cared? She raised the collar of her jacket against the rain and hustled to the studio as quick as she could in wool socks and Crocs.

Rahim had been an unexpectedly good hire. She scanned the pink sticky notes he'd stuck to the front of the desk-cabinet. The first one said, 'Don't touch my bench. I've got it.' Nice to see some confidence. She'd touch it anyway. It was her name on the website. She took a scan around the studio. They'd moved into this larger space six months... goodness, thought Vic, it's been a year. Twelve months in what she still thought of as the 'lux version', ten metres by five with a row of windows above eye level along the long wall. It had taken all of a week to spread out in the new space. Her workbench had grown into a series of worktables, plus an extra bench a little apart for Rahim's projects. Which reminded her, what was he working on, anyway?

She took a visual inventory of the power tools cluttering the far corner, a mismatched collection of plastic boxes and custom stands. Hard to tell what he'd been using, everything nicely put away. Near the door, they had created a sales office by slapping an Ikea rug in front of a recycled desk. Three well-used office chairs and a wilted palm gave shape to the public area. Never enough natural light to keep the thing happy. The remaining wall space was concealed by racks of parts. The lower shelves held pre-cut pieces, hardware, unfinished drawers, and odds-and-ends. Too much junk to tell what's missing. She left it to Rahim to track inventory these days. Neatly stacked long beams of wood filled the uppermost racks, fit for a boathouse worth of racing shells.

As long as she could remember, her personal life had been an unstoppable comic tragedy, a boulder of chaos tumbling down a mountain with her flat-footed in its path. So much of her time wasted dodging hard turds of dismay in the form of idiot boyfriends. Yet her art had always been orderly. At home, her clothes unfurled majestically across the downstairs rooms in a tornado of disarray. At work? She glanced at the cutlery drawer of their improvised desk. Her pencils for the next design were regimentally stowed. She picked up the second note. 'Call for materials. 044...' followed by something illegible. Rahim was better at furniture making than note taking. No matter. She kept a list of her supplier details in a spreadsheet. Shouldn't be too hard to match a number to Rahim's scrawl.

Her phone rang as she was booting the laptop. Unknown caller. Two years ago, that would have been a swift 'call declined'. Running a small business had changed her habits. Could be a customer, even if it was more likely a solicitation for a time share, or something else you'd only buy when pressured. Leg hair bleaching?

Not exactly her skin tone of thing. She stabbed the accept button. "Hello?"

"Well, how do, Miss Vic-tor-ee-ya." An unmistakable drawl.

"Dan!"

"Yes, ma'am, Dan's your man. On the horn, if not in the flesh. Have you heard from your momma?"

"What? Why on earth would I talk to her?" asked Vic.

"Jus' wonderin', is all. But never mind that. I got news."

"Yes, I'm also very well, how kind of you to ask." Vic paused. "What sort of news, exactly?"

"The good kind, angel. I got 'em."

"Got what?"

"The last wight. Found him in Moscow, in one of them boutique hotels. Zapped him but good. Caused a bit of a stink, seeing how he hadn't yet paid his bill. But I took care of it, and now I'm free to resume my carefree normal life."

"You mean, that's it? They're all gone?" Vic slumped onto the IKEA carpet, her back against the cabinet frame. "We're done? I can take the necklace off?"

"Well, I got twenty people in Bangalore with names I can't pronounce searchin' the hyper-global-mega-net for signs of any more of them critters. So far, ain't heard a peep. I reckon that was the last one. Got lucky. Caught up to him right before he was about to run off. Had a cute lil' duffel bag packed and all. New passport too. Jus' another missin' person now, so to speak."

Vic had unconsciously put one hand on her heart. She fingered the solid shape of the necklace under the fleece. "Oh, Dan, this is very good news. I'm afraid it might take me a moment to process."

"Take all the time you want, Miss Vicky. You're a free lady. But I do have one request. Assumin' you're willin' to do a favour for me, that is."

"Of course, Dan. How can I help?"

"You know how I'd said I got the last one?"

"Yes. About ten seconds ago." said Vic. She gathered herself into a half-kneel by the desk. Where was this going?

"Well, that wasn't exactly one hundert percent veracious. There's one more."

"Where?"

"Not where. Who," replied Dan. "Your brother."

Vic couldn't prevent a sharp intake of breath. "Phillip? He's safely tucked away in dream land with Mother dearest."

"That's right. But he ain't gonna be there forever. I got a hunch he's itchin' to come back. And if there's one thing I know about Lilith, it's that she can't deny that boy a thing. Now, if he comes back, he's likely to make more of those nasty creatures. Which will put you in danger and me back in a business I'd rather not have to be in, if you know what I mean. Oil and technology is more than a handful already. You wouldn't believe how badly a company runs when the H-M-F-I-C is off gallivantin'."

"The H-what?" asked Vic.

"Never mind, ain't fit talk for polite company." Dan's accent made it PO-lite.

"Fine, we're very polite," said Vic. "But I don't see how I can help with Phillip."

"Not the boy. I need your help with Lilith."

"My mother?" asked Vic. "I'd rather not."

"Well, hang on there, pardner. No need to get your panties all twisted 'round the axle. Here's the grift. Phillip is dangerous, if he comes back on his own. And he's also in danger, being a wanted man and all. I want to cut a deal with the devil's mother, so to speak. Get word to your mama. Tell her I'll sort out Phillip's legal contretemps", which sounded in Dan's mouth like 'con-tray-tomps', "and in exchange, Phillip will agree to not use magic."

"He'll never agree. And neither will I. He's a killer."

"Well, look here, Miss Vicky," said Dan. "As a judge of horseflesh, I outrank you by several hundred years. I've seen your brother's type before. Magic is a good game, I'll give you that. But his kind want power more than anything else. And money and high office will be more than enough substitute for the juice I want him to give up. Anyhoo, you leave that part to me. Just talk to your mother."

Vic stood up, pushing off the desk with her free hand. "I don't think I will. And even if I wanted to, I wouldn't know how."

"Damn it, woman. She's the Queen of the god-damn night. And you're her daughter. Call out to her as you're falling asleep. Unlike for me, she's always listening out for you." The line went dead.

Vic put her phone down on the desk. She walked past her workbench and sat down in an empty corner. Done. Done with fear, done with literally waiting for the beast in the night to return, done with wondering if the pale git on the bus in the Army surplus was sent to kill her, or simply an escapee from Glasgow. Or perhaps only almost done. She held her face in her hands for a moment and rubbed her eyes. Was she really going to help Dan bring her murderous brother back into the real world? She went back to the desk and picked up the phone.

– § –

George poked the chicken with a fork. "It's stuck."

Fatima didn't budge. "I told you to line the tray with aluminium foil."

"I know," he replied, shaking his head. "Now you'll remind me that–"

She didn't let him finish. "Recipes are the one place on the Internet where you SHOULD read the comments."

George removed the sheet pan from the oven with thick pink silicone gloves. "Voila," he said. "Chicken-au-sheet." Fatima straightened herself off the couch and moved to the dining room table, adjusting the trivet on the way. The wide tray barely fit around the place settings, in part because of the spoon embedded in the table centre. George turned to fetch a pair of oven tongs, holding up a hand to forestall the usual armada of words. Fatima watched him return to the table in silence, fork raised. "I'd like to name him after my father," he said.

Fatima put her fork down. "How do you know it's going to be a boy?" she asked. "And why do you get to decide?"

"I'm not deciding. I'm saying, I'd like it." George crossed his arms and leaned away from the table. "What name would you like?"

"I'd like to know first if it's a boy or a girl. Or maybe we give it something gender-neutral, like Dylan or Alex.

That way if they feel differently, no inconvenience."

"I think by the time they're an adult, they can choose whatever name they want."

"Again, the assumptions, George. People come out around puberty. The median age that kids know is around twelve. What if..."

"What if we don't have a healthy baby? Isn't it a bit early to think about sexuality?"

"God, George. It's thoughts like that which make me want to have a cigarette."

George smacked the table, scalding the edge of his hand on the sheet pan. He looked at Fatima, guilty hand in mouth. After a moment's suck, he popped the injured hand out. "You're only saying that to wind me up," he said.

"Somewhat," admitted Fatima. "But it's better we have this out properly between the two of us than in front of your mum."

George puffed out a conciliatory breath. "You're not wrong about that." Fatima's phone interrupted whatever he was going to say next. 'Holler', by the Spice Girls.

"Sounds like Vic," said Fatima. She leaned over to grab her phone from the couch and fell out of her chair. George shot out of his own chair and scrabbled at Fatima on the ground.

She propped herself on an elbow, half-hidden by the

table. "George, my idiot prince, can you reach the phone? On the couch. I'm fine. Twasn't much of a drop."

George bustled to the phone, finding the speaker button. "Vic?"

"George?" Vic sounded slightly husky on the speaker. "Is Fatima there?"

"Yes," he said. "You're on speaker."

"What's up?" Fatima went from spilled-out-of-the-chair to full lying-on-the-floor. She held out her hands for George to drag her back to the couch.

"He did it, Fatima," said Vic, from the couch speaker.

"Who did what, Vixen?" asked Fatima. George tugged at her raised hand without success. He moved the phone off the couch and grabbed her with both hands.

"Got the last wight. Dan. He's killed them all."

"Oof. One second, Vic." George lifted Fatima. She gave him a quick kiss, then got them situated, pulling George down so that they sat together with the phone in her lap. "OK, sorry about that. Logistics. What were you saying?"

"I'm saying that I don't have to worry anymore about getting eaten by beasties in the night. Dan called me. He found the last one in Russia and....well, I'm not sure what he did, but he's assured me that it's gone. It's dead."

"That's excellent news. I mean, not that we should be

taking much joy in the killing of things, but that was certainly one creature that needed a killing." Fatima beat a drum solo on the arm of the couch. "You're sure that's it?" she asked.

"As sure as one can be with this kind of business. Apparently, he has some team of programmers searching the Internet for clues. Nothing found."

"That's not precisely comforting. George finds nothing on the Internet all the time, and he's not satisfied."

"I thought his satisfaction was your job," replied Vic. George quietly turned pink.

"Not at all, Vixen. We're a modern couple. If he can't learn to take care of himself, well then, what have I married? But tell me more," continued Fatima. "You think it's really over?"

"I do and I don't. I need a second opinion. Or even a third."

"About what?"

"I think the ghouls are dealt with. But Dan asked me to talk to my mother…" Vic's voice trailed off.

Fatima slapped the couch arm again. "Are you trying to keep us in suspense? Talk about what?"

Vic coughed. "About Phillip. Dan wants him to come back."

"Why on earth would anyone want that?"

"To make a deal. He's worried that Phillip will come back and pick up his old trade. And if Phillip does that, he might make a new wight by accident. Which will put us right back to where we were." Vic went quiet, but Fatima outwaited her. "So," Vic continued, "Dan is offering a deal. If Phillip will agree not to use magic, Dan will sort his legal trouble and restart his political career."

"Oh," replied Fatima. Vic could picture her wrinkled forehead of surprise. "And exactly how would Dan do that?"

"I imagine with his millions," said Vic.

"Hundreds of millions," cut in Fatima. "I think Dan has the kind of wealth that can buy you out of anything. Impunity money."

Vic couldn't help but laugh at the turn of phrase. "Impunity money? Is that higher or lower than crazy rich?"

"Higher," replied Fatima. "It's the kind of money that turns murders into misunderstandings." She put her hand over George's on the couch. "Vix, I've seen this type of money in action. You need to be bloody careful. I'm not sure if helping Dan bring Phillip back is a good idea."

"Yeah, Fats, me neither. That's why I called. But I'm also not excited about the idea of Phillip returning at the time and place of his choosing. I'm worried he's going to start the whole nasty game up all over again, no matter what I do. I'm leaning towards trying."

"Trying to talk to your mother? Did he give you any tips on how exactly you could pull that off?"

Vic snorted. "Not really. But she is indeed my mother. When can you come to Bristol? I think it's time to take a scary nap in a chalk circle again."

IF THOU BE KING, WHERE IS THY CROWN?

Josh gets an upgrade, Vic gets distracted

DeVilliers sat behind the desk of the Sellen & Sellen senior partner and ran his hand over the polished wood. He had stopped working from home first, more than a year ago. Why not take Hugh's office? It was the nicest.

He felt less an imposter each day, even if he sometimes worried he was wearing shoes a size too big. Hugh had vanished shortly before the pandemic. Josh had been on holiday, as instructed. It had carried a bit of mystery until Mrs. Evans discovered an 'in the event of' document filed with the partnership papers in a neglected cabinet. Dated about six months before Hugh's disappearance, it was in two parts. The second part was a brief codicil authorising any partner who wished, junior or otherwise, to take over the practice by paying a substantial, but not prohibitive, lump sum into a trust previously established by Hugh. The first part was a meandering preamble enumerating Hugh Sellen's deeply felt misgivings about becoming a lawyer, his long-suppressed wish to return to the pursuits of his youth, and a handwritten coda that stated 'if you find me suddenly gone, it simply means I've had it. You'd do well to start searching in Paris, but by the time you begin, I'll be in the wind.'

Hugh was divorced. His father, the older and perhaps more famous half of the firm's name, long dead. Hugh might have had some issues, but no children. No attachments at all, other than the firm. Josh often wondered if Hugh had a premonition of the public health emergency to come. Maybe he had simply hit some internal limit, felt it was time. Regardless, he was gone and the firm rudderless. The other two junior solicitors weren't interested in running things. Josh talked it over with his wife. They re-mortgaged the house, and with a little help from her parents, bought out Hugh's share.

He decided to keep the name. What was the use of owning a business that no one knew to hire? Perhaps in a few years they might change it to Sellen & DeVilliers. Or DeVilliers, Sellen & Sellen. Something. His name first felt right. He liked being in charge. He had a knack for it. When the world shifted online, Josh was ready. Billable hours up thirty percent, it was time to take on another lawyer, perhaps expand into criminal cases. But some cases still needed to be handled by the head of the firm. Which was him, now. Personally. Like the Sberbank file.

Josh had been surprised to find Sberbank was the only file Hugh had been billing. Sellen had given over all his other work to the juniors. Well, mostly, Hugh had given it to him. Josh removed the lever arch file from his top drawer. Perhaps Hugh shedding workload had been in anticipation of his departure. Or of shedding something else. Hugh and Josh had worked reasonably closely on the Sberbank engagement, but there were still a few startling details he'd discovered in Hugh's copy of the file. And some nasty messages in Hugh's email account. Another privilege of becoming the owner, access to the firm's servers. Correspondence that included a disturbing warning note to the daughter of a client whose will Hugh had handled himself. That was unusual. Josh rubbed his face. He was wasting time musing. What to do about this new enquiry? Why would anyone other than Sberbank want to hire him to safeguard Sberbank accounts?

– § –

Vic looked up from her rabbit-hole of spreadsheets and noticed it was night. Enough streetlight leaked through the clerestory that she often forgot to turn on the studio overheads. She stood up from the computer, eyes smarting, and flicked the switches by the door. The change in brightness lifted her mood. Enough computer work, she thought. The emails she'd been avoiding could wait a bit longer. Time to see how the apprentice was coming along.

Her normal checking on Rahim's work in progress was now too often being diverted by what she and Rahim had taken to calling 'the Throne'. It was really the only way to describe it. They had started the project a few months ago. Rahim had been working late, finishing a Modern Legends side table, so they were both at the studio. It had started raining. Vic decided to call it an early-ish night. Her excuse was to give him a ride home. They had almost reached his family's house in the lanes behind Barton Hill when their path was blocked by a downed tree.

An ancient black walnut leant across the road. A minor spring shower had brought down a monarch. What had lived through years of gale force winds and urban development was brought low by a quirk of a wind gust. Low, yet revenged, its crown of branches crumpling the roof of an unlucky Ford Fiesta. It lay against the Ford in downward dog, attended by a cluster of Fire & Rescue in fluorescent orange. A lone figure lay flares in the wet. The others stood in a circle, discussing how to remove it.

It had been an odd day in many respects. Vic had started with an unusually long dive. Not that she was on to something. Tristan, one of the swimmers at the boat club, had loaned her an extra oxygen cylinder. He was one of the strivers "on the cusp". On the cusp of being able to quit his day job, on the cusp of being in the top ten British triathletes, with a few backers and a good chance at a personal best this year that might push him into the elite ranks. On the cusp meant stitching together random gear underwriters. Tristan's suit sponsor was trying to break into the diving market. In exchange for free kit, he was supposed to review their gear. He'd kept the neoprene hood and the gloves, and asked Vic to ghostwrite about the tank. What could go wrong?

The extra kilos of aluminium the sponsor added to the bottom might have made the cylinder more neutral in water, but they cost Vic an extra fifteen minutes of fumbling with unfamiliar weight. Worth it for another hour of diving. She still had bars left after three hours, but the extended period of breathing bottled air gave her a furry tongue and a sore throat. Worse, there was no proper way to tie a third cylinder down in the van. She ended up leaving it strapped into her buoyancy jacket, wedged as best she could against the chainsaw case.

The chainsaw itself was overdue at Brandon Hire Station. It was poor planning (Rahim's words) or complete luck (Vic's) that they still had it in the van. She'd rented it the previous day when she and Rahim had tried to deliver a custom chaise to a second-floor address. It had slipped Vic's mind that the delivery fee she'd negotiated included removal of the old sofa. That thing turned out to be a Chesterfield, complete with arms fully rolled up an extravagant back. Rahim reckoned the battleship had most likely reached its port by hoist. Either that, or it was original to the once grand house's construction. Which was possible – the battered black velvet probably started life a fine hunter green. The two of them certainly couldn't carry it down the narrow stairway created when the mansion was chopped into flats. As the mansion, so too its sofa, Vic decided. They called the hire centre.

She'd opened a trade account when she'd taken on Rahim so that he could experiment with reciprocating saws and angle grinders without destroying hers. Forty minutes later, Rahim was carrying manageable cuts of velvet and beech down the stairs. It would have been faster if Vic's safety goggles hadn't kept fogging up.

Should have known a storm was coming.

After staring at the downed tree through the windscreen for a dozen beats of the wipers, she reluctantly sent Rahim out in the wet to offer their help. By the time the fire brigade said yes, she had a plan. The trunk was a metre in diameter. Her van was empty, but for the diving gear and its wonky cylinder.

Two wet and sweaty hours later, she dropped an exhausted Rahim at his door, with a promise to help her carry the salvaged stump up to the studio later. Overnight, it could sit stowed inside the van. Clearly, hardwood and stairs would be a continuing theme.

The next day they discovered a champion block of wood. "Championly heavy", remarked Rahim. After circumnavigating it four times, Vic proposed to make a chair. It would be a solid chair, carved out of the stump in a single piece. They'd remove the wood between four flowing legs, grind out a flat seat, and leave a half-ring of solid wood from which to carve the arms and back. If they did it right, the chair would reveal itself within the truncated bole of hard walnut.

The first day they stripped off the bark and stopped. They'd make trial cuts in a soft pine facsimile. Which started a lumberyard odyssey – three pine blocks, similar in size to the black stump, crisscrossed with chalk marks and exploratory cuts.

Their first attempt was a disaster. The legs were elegant but too thin in proportion to the seat. That pine made a cheery blaze in Vic's dad's fireplace. Her fireplace. In her house. They got the design right with the second, but a moment's inattention put a hole in what was planned to be a continuous fold of wood along the back. Which was why they had started with pine in the first place. No shortage of firewood that season.

The third came out so well, they stained and lacquered it, despite knowing the soft pine would mark. It made for a beautifully marketed architectural piece on the Victoria Ali Bespoke website. More importantly, they had a life model for the real work of cutting and shaping hard walnut.

The difference in density meant that the real stump was slow to yield the throne. Its promise distracted Vic, throbbed in the corner of her mind like a siren. Alone at night in the studio, she should probably do anything other than fuss with it. Sod it. She hauled at the painter's cloth covering the part-hewn block. There was a pink post-it note taped securely to the hollow of the roughed-in seat. 'Check your email,' in Rahim's handwriting. Vic laughed. He really does know me.

She left the dust cloth on the floor and stalked back

to the computer desk. OTP, OTP, click here to resend text message. How did they know her phone number? Or had she given her phone with her email account? She couldn't remember. Either way, the text message was ages in coming. She had almost given up waiting when the ping came. Twelve digits! Must be important. Vic carefully punched the numbers into the email dialog. The locked envelope icon dissolved into Arial text. She belatedly checked the 'from' address: friend8247y-42323-358098@gmail.com. As if that didn't scream shady. Her eye caught on the salutation. 'Dear Victoria Emir Ali'. Who called her that? Too late to un-click, might as well read the thing:

Dear Victoria Emir Ali,

You know me as Reggie, but in truth, I've had many names and lives. Many, but not enough. That you are reading this message means I am dead, only a few years since we first met. Perhaps you are the unluckiest charm of all.

After the film hall, I had still hoped the plan might work. When the vote failed, I laid low in England. Freddie had to pay. Then I turned to you. Or I would have, but for the lockdown. Documentation cost me the best part of a year. By the time I arranged a vaccination record, Dan had found me. He watched me stalk your house and warned me off but let me live. I fled to Russia. Easier than England, but expensive.

My Russian friends gave me a new name but would not hide me for long. They were more afraid of Daniel than me. Which makes sense, since Daniel is the same as I. Except, more money.

In exchange for removing the problem of myself from Moscow, Arkady promised to send this mail one month from my last contact. Sometime in the last month I breathed my last. You would not believe how hard that phrase is to write. You would not believe how many days I have walked the Earth, how many breaths have already expired. I am greedy for new ones yet. But not so greedy that I won't offer you advice. Do not trust Dan. That which prolongs our lives has a flavour. A scent, you might say. Dan reeks of it. Man, not oil. I know this flavour well. Do no favours for him. It will end in a killing.

-Roman

Vic reread the message. If it was fake, someone had put in an awful amount of effort. She closed the laptop. There was a loud pop outside, followed by darkness.

This current version of Vic was no scared waif. Nothing to be afraid of. The streetlamp that turned her twilight sodium orange had blown. Coincidence. Time I should be going as well, she thought. Not a great email. Not a great night to be alone. She grabbed her jacket, swapped her sandals for the trainers she kept under the shelf, turned off the overheads, and stepped out into the dark.

The door of The White Hart opened into a crowded main room, surprisingly crowded after, well, the pandemic. 'Masks make for hard drinking' was painted on the oar hung from one of the dark beams overhead. A wood paneled bar ran most of the length of the long room. Vic could hardly see the bar through an array of prodigious torsos. It was as if the pub had been invaded by a mob of prop forwards and professional wrestlers. Track suits and hoodies were the order of the day, a very large number of which were silk-screened with barbell icons. In the before times, this many large men would have spiked her 'stranger danger' sensor. She crossed the threshold anyway.

After two years of hardly going out, the radar was out of practice, wasn't it? Besides, her risk-reward equation was all skewed. She rescanned the room. Maybe with less youth came more foolish. Besides, it wasn't a complete 'blokes night out'. There was an occasional female standee at the bar and scattered at the high-top tables. Perhaps one is to two, although these ladies were reasonably matched in size to the men. Wouldn't need a taxi if their bloke fell over. They'd simply carry him home on one shoulder.

Vic spotted a normal-sized fellow wedged between two mountains of humanity, tailored suit doubly incongruous amongst XXL athletic gear. He was talking earnestly to one of the prop forwards. Excited hand-waving and the occasional slap on the back. Must be some muscle on that little frame; the smaller man was hardly staggered by the return pounding of his drinking mate, who picked that moment to abandon the bar. Must need a toilet the size of a bathtub, thought Vic. She slid into the vacated spot. "Mind if I squeeze in for a moment?", she asked. It was hardly a squeeze. You could have fit a London bus in the gap.

Close quarters revealed a wispy moustache, more mouse than 'stache. Moustache gave her a side look and a nod. "Tracy will be some time." The side look lingered, then morphed into a sadly standard and mildly creepy up-and-down. "Welcome to the party. In fact, let me buy you a drink." He waved at the bartender. "Maddie? She's with us."

Vic gave her own wave at the bartender, keeping her arm raised while turning to her new companion. "I can buy my own drinks, thanks."

"Right, right, wouldn't imply." He held out a slim-wristed hand as a peace offering. "Fabio."

"Victoria."

"Like Beckham, except with a hint of Scary."

Vic batted Fabio's hand away. "For that, you CAN pay for my drink." She turned to the bartender. "Double Oban."

"Ouch," replied Fabio. "Good thing I'm Fabiolus."

Vic raised an eyebrow. "Fabiolus?"

"My nom de party. We're here to have a fabulously good time. Hence, Fabiolus."

"Fine," said Vic. "I'll bite. What's the occasion?"

Fabio pointed with his chin. "Archie over there, brother of our friend Tracy, just won Britain's Strongest Man."

"Ah. Some kind of weight-lifting competition?" asked Vic.

Fabio sprayed his sip of beer. "Some kind?" He put his pint on the bar and dabbed at Vic's jacket with a handkerchief. "It's only the most important strength event in the UK. Qualifier for World's Strongest Man. The most prestigious reality television athletic event on the Internet."

"Congrats to Archie," said Vic, "although that does feel a bit like 'winner-in-the-category-I've-defined-for-myself'.

Fabio shrugged. "If your category win is worth several million pounds. Hence," a dip of the handkerchief to the returning bartender, "your free drink."

"Thank you." A wave of people rippled around the small mountain making its way back to the bar. "That must be Tracy."

"It is, indeed. Shall we give the brother-of-the-king

some room, and find a table?"

Moments like this were telegrams from the future. Later, she'd likely wonder what she'd been thinking, in saying 'yes'. Increasingly, though, Vic was finding that how her future self might feel was a less reliable guide to the present than it used to be. It wasn't that she made less mistakes, although she did. It was more that she didn't need to learn as much from them. Future-self gave fewer fucks than before. The imperfections of her present self were something with which she had become, what was that word? Comfortable.

INCONCLUSIONS

George finds a fortune. Vic takes a number, then gets spooked

"Mrs. Fatima." George was working on something, his laptop on the dining table.

"Yes, my prince?" replied Fatima, languid on the sofa.

"You remember those two Russians with the guns?" asked George.

"You mean the ones who shot you?" Fatima raised up slightly. "Yes, I do believe I remember. Your blood, my dismay, that one?"

George gave a dismissing flick of the hand. "Not that. You remember that they were supposed to be bank employees, right?"

"Sounds about right."

"But they were brought up on gun charges. Not financial crimes."

"I think when the police arrest you for shooting up the ferry pier, a prosecution on gun crimes feels like the correct order of the day. I imagine there were enough gun charges to put them away for decades. I doubt a QC is going to waste time looking for hard-to-prove stuff when they have video footage of you machine gunning a police skiff, now would they?"

"Fair cop. But I've been messaging Cisco Stu. The programmer."

"Your hacker friend."

"Really Emir Ali's, but, sure, my hacker friend. It seems the money never went away."

Fatima took her legs off the couch and sat straight. "What do you mean, the money never went away?"

"The Russians had transferred enough money to buy a bank. It's still there. They used Ethereum. In other words, blockchain. Anyone can look up the transactions, view the ledger entries, money in and out of an account. It's all. Still. There. Been on a bit of a wild ride. At one point, they could have bought all of Barclays. Now it's more like a small to medium building society."

"That would still be a healthy sum."

"Indeed. More than a billion pounds."

"What is it sitting around for?"

"Wish I knew, love, wish I knew."

Fatima curled her knees beneath her chin. "Can we find out?"

– § –

Fabio steered Vic to a two-seater banquette in the room off the main bar. Quieter, although Britain's strongest men were always going to be audible. And getting more so with each round. Fabio slid a beer mat in front of the seat next to Vic. She nodded at the empty chair opposite. Fabio shrugged. "Don't feel like shouting across the table. Cheers." He clinked his glass against Vic's and took a deep sip. "So," he continued, "obvious questions first. What's a nice girl like you wandering in here for?"

"What makes you think I'm nice?" asked Vic. "And if we're being obvious, what's a small fellow like you doing with that lot?"

"Fair," replied Fabio. "But I do work out. A lot. I might not have the size, but I have the strength." He pushed his jacket sleeve up his wrist. It stopped abruptly on a cone-shaped forearm. "Took some doing to get a jacket that rests this nicely," he said, smoothing the rumpled cuff. "Met Trace at the gym. He and Arch were stacking so many plates, they needed two spotters. We'd been nodding acquaintances for some time. Serious lifters don't talk much, but they knew I was regular. They knew me. And so. It came out that they were training for the competition. And I was an agent." Fabio made a 'voila' gesture.

"Makes sense. But what were you training for?"

"Me? Nothing special - trying to get bigger. But I don't have the chemistry."

"You mean steroids?"

"No, no, definitely no. Archie and Tracy are 100% natural." Fabio underlined the negative with an emphatic head shake. "I meant testosterone. I got on the pills late."

"I'm not sure I follow," said Vic.

Fabio touched his mustache. "I was a woman before the pandemic. Hence the stubbornly skinny wrists. Lesbian for years, and heavy gym work changed my shape some time back. But I didn't have the courage to go 'outdoors' as a man. At some point, you get tired of wearing ambiguous clothes, pretending you're one thing when you're not. But I came late to the chemical party. How do you explain to your colleagues that from today, you're a man? Call me by a new name?"

"I thought people were doing that all the time now."

"Now! They're a bit younger than I am. And it's bloody hard. My gay friends used to tell me, 'Everyone under 35 already came out to their parents. Over 35, not so much.'"

"Which is a big joke, as everyone knows," said Vic.

"A big sad joke. They know, and they don't want to

know. Because it's easier to pretend your son might marry a woman, someday, than to deal with things you don't like. And the son gets reminded every day that his parents are SO disgusted, they'd rather pretend to believe something obviously untrue than accept their own child. Everyone knows." Fabio paused for a sip. "Although it looks like I had you fooled."

"You did." Vic smiled. "I think it was the gross leer and the chat up. Very convincing."

"It should be. I'm genuinely interested."

"Thanks," said Vic. "But don't be offended if I'm curious for something different." Vic pursed her lips.

"Go on, then," said Fabio.

"You sure? Stop me if I go too far." She centered her whisky glass in its damp ring. "How did you do it?"

"Switch? Go trans?"

"Yeah," replied Vic. "I mean, I was fooled. Or perhaps fooled is the wrong word. I mean, who exactly am I talking to?"

"Fabio!" The hard line forming on Fabio's mouth softened. "The one and only. Not the book cover model, of course. Couldn't stand having hair that long. The agent version. A good one."

"Yes, yes," said Vic. "So. How?"

"Middle of lockdown, it was all video calls with the camera off, right? I figured I could try it."

"And how did THAT go?" Vic stopped. "Wait. I don't mean to be obnoxious. Too much? Offensive?"

"Somewhat. I'm used to it. Besides, you're old enough to know better, but cute enough to get away with it."

"You really ARE a man."

"In every way but the sausage."

"Ha! A man with terrible lines. Does anyone actually say things like that?"

"Ah, Victoria, what's a trans-boy to do? I'm making this up as I go. How would YOU know what it is to be a man? And then you get on the hormones, and it's like 'woah, NOW I get what the testicle carriers go through.' Took a long time to tame the mood swings. And the aggro. Gave me some sympathy for the boys. Makes the camaraderie easier."

"I bet. Seems a hard way to get it."

"It was the right way for me. And it's still a work in progress."

"Well," said Vic, "in the come-on department, you're quite advanced. Which I must say is a bit of a surprise to me. Don't you remember what it was like to be a woman, getting hit on by some creep?"

"Sure, but kind of a yes-and-no." Fabio wavered a hand back and forth. "I was always a bit butch. Had that 'other vibe'. Guys didn't really try too much on with me, before. To your point, what I find strange is that I DO remember, and I kind of don't care. Being a bit forward is effective. I mean, there's a part of me that feels like I'm betraying all women, but it works."

"Ugh," said Vic. "Depressing, but credible." Her glass was empty. She looked at Fabio. "So how did it go? I really am curious."

"The swap of Anna for Fabio?"

"Anna?" asked Vic.

"Yeah, Fab Anna, life of the party, DJ in the dj, short-haired girl in men's jackets, friend to all, lover to not very many. Her? How did I swap out her?"

"Exactly. Sounds like I would have liked her."

"Which makes sense, since you like me." Fabio tented hands in front of his mouth. Vic kept her face neutral. "Well," he continued, "it was like any crisis. Slowly, then all at once. I got on the hormone patches. In a few weeks, you could hear the change. My throat got a bit scratchy, my voice got deeper. Not enough to make people mistake it was me, but noticeable." Fabio touched his temples. "The hair loss was the worst. They warn you about it, but the male pattern baldness was still a shock. And also the point. You can't be a man without the male."

"Then you told your family, your colleagues, call me Fabio?"

"Yeah, not quite. My parents were fine. They kind of

gave up on dreams for their little girl when I came out as queer. Colleagues? Couldn't build up the nerve to break it directly to the people at the agency. I could handle reactions from strangers. Playing the repulsion lottery with my co-workers, that felt a bit too much. I quit. Started my own firm. Asked my existing accounts if they wanted to be repped by the new me. The boy-me."

"And?"

"And money talks. They knew I was a good agent, would do right by them. I lost a few, mostly because they were loyal to the old firm, not because they were bigots. Updated my LinkedIn profile. Changed the email signature. This is year two of AF Agencies."

"Agencies?"

"Yeah, plural. I knew from the start I'd be multi-corporated. Another one of the great things about being a man in real life. Nobody questions your ambition. Speaking of which, you want to get out of here?"

"I do, Fabio. But I think I'll head off alone." Vic rose from the table. "I came out because I wanted to get some unsettling news off my mind. You've been excellent in that regard, but it's time I went home."

"Wait. I'd like to see you again." Fabio took a slim wallet from his jacket. "Let me give you my card, at least."

Vic disappeared the pastel card with a sly hand. Been

a while, she thought.

"What just happened?" asked Fabio.

Vic re-appeared the card with a flick of her fingers, then banished it again. "My father was a magician." She tapped at the top of the card, now snug in Fabio's breast pocket.

"That's cool." Fabio touched his jacket pocket. The card wasn't there. "Neat. What other hobbies do you have up your sleeve?"

Hobbies? Time to go, she thought. "Thank you for the drink." Vic turned at the door and gave him a salute, his business card a pastel flag between her fingers.

$$- \S -$$

Fatima's voice was thick with sleep. "Vicky, you can't do this to me now. I don't keep these hours anymore."

"Fats, it's hardly midnight. On a Friday. It's not even eleven." Vic tossed the van keys on the kitchen counter. "Pubs are still open."

"And I'm a married pregnant cow. We need our beauty sleep." Fatima half-rolled out of bed, waking George. "It's just Vics, go back to bed," she whispered.

"Actually, I need him too," Vic continued. "Good thing you didn't turn off your phone."

"And let YOU go to voicemail. I'd never."

"Thank you, darling." Vic rucked a shoe off with the heel of her other foot. "Think of this as sleep deprivation training for when the parasite breaches."

"Oh, there's a lovely thought, Vixen. And we were going to make you a godparent."

"You must. But first I need your help." Vic dislodged the other shoe and paced the length of the kitchen cabinets in her socks. "And George."

"About what?" asked Fatima. She lifted herself into a sitting position, one hand over her belly. "You're sounding awful cool for this time of night. I don't hear emergency. Can't it wait until we come down to Bristol for the séance?"

"Yes and no. Although I may have found a fifth for the pentagram. Pentacle. The damn star on the floor." Vic picked her key ring off the counter. "But I need some advice now." She ran a thumb over the alarm button on the fob. "In fact, I think I've already wasted a few hours of head start."

"Ok, Vixen. Spill it. What have you been waiting on?"

Vic stopped pacing her kitchen. "I got one of those emails. That George is always warning us to pay attention to. I need to know if it's real."

Fatima sat up straighter, moving the support arm from her belly to her back. "One of those emails? Let me put you on speaker. Hang on." She elbowed George and dropped the phone on the bed. "Georgie, it's the village idiot. She needs help. Again."

Driving the electric van at night still took her some getting used to. The instrument cluster glowed like the spaceship consoles on the television of her youth. 24,867 miles. Soon to be 25,000. Which had included more than a few hours in the dark. The vision was fine. LED headlights were brilliant. It was the soundtrack. Even normally at night, sound took on a new character. The revs of her too-brief motorcycle career had always been a welcome companion in the dark. The EV motor made almost no sound, especially on the motorway. In a funny way it was more normal when it rained. The wipers, the need for more concentration on the road, you didn't miss the buzz of the engine. On clear nights like tonight, the low electric hum was swamped by the noise of wheels on tarmac. She wasn't tired. It was hardly midnight, after all. But something more than the occasional brief rumble of expansion joints would have been welcome.

Vic grimaced into the windscreen. I guess I've lived with creeping death long enough to need more stimulation, she thought. Or maybe we've all become impatient in the pandemic. More, now, everything. Except the task at hand. Vic turned off the phone nav.

She pondered how she might get to Fatima's without it.

It was Fatima's idea that Vic come to their flat. Mostly untraceable, even if Vic knew the way. George practiced a vigorous digital hygiene. He used his mum's address for all correspondence. Took some doing, but he'd convinced Fatima to do the same. 'Gives her something to do', he'd said, somewhat ungenerously. His mother did enjoy the errand, having reason to call almost daily. That had its pluses and minuses.

Fatima, like most practicing journos, had a vigorous Twitter habit, or rather, the app formerly known as Twitter. She also didn't mind a bit of the Insta, which she wasn't going to give up. Every two weeks or so, George would search for the end of the Internet. He'd eliminate as best he could any links or references to real addresses and biodata. The Google personal content removal request form had been in his favourites for years.

Some leakage couldn't be helped, but to the best of his paranoid standards, their flat was 'off net'. For £350 a year in company formation fees, the lease was through the UK subsidiary of a made-up-but-legal US corporation, registered to a post office box in Nevada. Fatima had been appalled. "Why would we ever want to do business in Vegas? Or even visit?" After the seventh time he assured her of his complete lack of desire to see the Britney Spears residency at Planet Hollywood, or any other residency for that matter, she'd let him manage the paperwork his way. In the future, he'd argued, everyone would have a Nevada company. Even if it meant George would never get to go to DefCon. Every marriage has its sacrifices.

A bleary-eyed George opened the door at half-four. "It's Saturday, Vic. Turn off the phone, come in and sleep. From what you've said, the thing has already kept a few days. You're unlikely to be found, here. Let's get some rest." George started up the stairs of the maisonette. "Fatima's asleep. I'm going back to bed as well."

"I'm a bit too wired, Georgie," replied Vic.

"Well, I'm too sleepy for detailed work. Give us a few hours. Maybe take a walk for a while?" George blushed. "I mean, you're welcome to hang about on the couch. There's a clean laptop you can use upstairs."

"More than fair, George. Sorry for ruining your Friday night kip. Saturday morning. I got a bit spooked when Fats said 'don't stay home'."

"Or anywhere else anyone would look for you. Which is apparently not 'in bed.'" George took another step up the stairs, then stopped. "Look, there's a lovely bakery about a mile down Broadway. It's a nice walk. You can read the fish wrappers. Perhaps even pick us up a bacon roll on the way back. But please, please, turn off your phone."

"Already did. And a walk is a fab idea." Vic grinned at the thought of 'Fab'. "Besides, one shouldn't wake a pregnant lady twice in one night. She'll get plenty of that soon enough." Vic handed her backpack up to George. "Ta, Georgie!" She waved at his retreating feet and closed the front door in the black before dawn. "Two bacon rolls, in a few hours' time," she whispered, an incantation. As if that would be enough to not bring anything more sinister back with her.

NO PLACE LIKE HOME

Families prove problematic, Dan loses a buff

Lilith raised her finger and the music stopped. The trumpet player rocked back and forth. The hands of the saxophonist writhed on buttons and levers. The bass player plucked away on the cabaret's small stage. Visually, it was an arresting performance – no sound came out. Lilith recrossed her legs, pivoting to face Phillip, the red underside of her heels gleaming in the dim salon. "I am so tired of hearing you say you want to go home." She drew a baton-like cigarette holder out of the onyx gem of the bangle on her left wrist. "This!" She thrust the cigarette holder at Phillip's face, a lit cigarette appearing on its tip. "This is the stuff of gods. Your home is here, in the heart of power."

Phillip licked his finger and extinguished the cigarette with a moist tip. "This is your place." He looked at the black char mark on his light brown finger. It became liquid and dripped away. "It has its appeal, true." He observed his mother. "But it is most definitely not home."

"Bah," replied Lilith. "Your home is here, in the unlimited kingdom." She pursed her lips and puffed out a small flame, relighting the cigarette. "Whatever you want, whatever you desire, anything you can imagine." She waved a tendril of smoke, "And it becomes. Here we sculpt in power." She gave a small nod of her chin to the silent band. The music returned, softer than before. "The things of the life you want are...what?" She asked. "A fancy car? A flash house? Apply your mind."

"Apply? That's just it," countered Phillip. "There are no other minds." He stood and rubbed his hands down the front of his dinner jacket. Sateen lapels rippled into an Aston Villa track suit. The jacket's black pearl buttons popped off, transforming into casino chips as they hit the floor. Phillip picked one up. "Here. Play this on red. Except it won't matter, because we ARE the house." Phillip breathed lightly on the £100 chip. It vanished in a small black cloud of soot, leaving the golden semicircle of a casino logo hanging in the air. "This is your place. My place is London. My HOME is London. And I want to go home."

"And you will, my son." Lilith wafted the soot back with an elegant hand. A restored casino chip spun suspended, gold letters winking. "In time."

"How much time, mother?" Phillip knocked the chip

out of the air. "You saw the note from Dan. There's no need to wait."

A dark suited waiter crossed the dance floor with a full cocktail tray. Lilith lifted a martini glass before reconsidering Phillip. "There was never any need to wait. So, they didn't. And they died." Lilith took a cool sip. "Dan has an agenda. He is on no side but his own."

"And I can help him."

"In exchange for giving up magic? For promising to never use magic on Earth again?" Lilith snorted. "You'd do that? And he'd believe it?"

"Yes. I would. Temporarily. For real power. Power in London. Power in the world." Phillip gestured the waiter for the second glass. "Dan needs help. He's rich, but he needs my friends. My political friends. Which will make us both billionaires. Billion. With a B."

Lilith glanced at one of the casino chips on the floor. It slid under the waiter's raised foot, skidding his shoe on the varnished dance floor. The second martini splashed across the front of Phillip's football kit. "I know a word that starts with B," said Lilith. "And it hangs around the arse end of a bull. Be very sure that's not what this is."

Phillip shook spray from his hands. The lion in his Aston Villa badge awakened. Its claret tongue stretched out and slurped the track suit dry. Phillip righted the glass in his lap, instantly refilled, and took a sip. "Then we are agreed," he said. "We should carefully consider Dan's offer."

– § –

George stood in the back of his van, smelling faintly of bacon roll, his face illuminated by monitors bolted to the parts racks. This is the worst, he thought. Scratch that. Telephone technical support for your friends was the worst. Customer support he could handle. Customers at least were paying. Somehow, the exchange of money made it less traumatic for people when things didn't work. My router has stopped working? Oh mate, that's rough. Guess you'll have to buy a new one. How much do they cost? That's customers. But friends. Stopped working? Can't you fix it? Isn't there something you can do? Not really, mate. If you were paying me, I could buy you a new one. You think I can work magic? As Vic keeps telling us, magic isn't real. Even if I've seen it with my own eyes.

George rubbed the place where his trousers covered the bullet scar. Still the idiot doing special missions for free, aren't I? He blew out his cheeks and checked the parts bin for a USB keyboard dongle. Should have bought Bluetooth, but I was on budget, wasn't I? USB caps all look the bloody same. Good thing he'd added a hub to his rackmount, lots of spare ports for testing.

After a few tries, George pecked at the big plastic keyboard and was rewarded with movement in the left monitor. At last. He rechecked the coax cable run through the small port in the back door. Its other end connected into the main Telecom box in Finchley. If only he could remember which directory he'd installed the Tor server in.

He shivered in his t-shirt inside the van. This will be much harder when the little one comes along. His mom had asked him, 'How do you think you'll cope?' It was meant in a loving way but felt like an accusation. That he wouldn't cope? People have done this for thousands of generations. It's not like we invented parenting. George puffed out a wry grunt. You might think otherwise by the way some of his colleagues went on, he thought. Their precious angels. Soon he'd have one of his own. Make it hard to hang around an obscure street corner, wire hanging out the arse of the van, trying to connect to a random email server, now, wouldn't it?

A very tired Vic swiveled towards the clatter of the lock like a flower seeking the sun. George's face brought more of a dark cloud to mind. "Nothing," he said.

"What do you mean, nothing?" Fatima asked, over her shoulder. She was lying on her back on the floor, legs propped up the wall. "It's supposed to be good for the baby," she said.

"Nothing," continued George. "You've heard of the Great Firewall of China?"

"Yes," replied both Fatima and Vic.

"Well, Russia has one too. Without the snappy name. Very hard to get through."

"You mean like the Iron Curtain?" asked Fatima.

"Precisely. Or the Iron Cyber-curtain. Where network packets go to die."

"You traced it to Russia," said Vic, standing up from the couch.

George held up both hands. "As far as Russia. Maybe further. Perhaps even much further, or just as likely, from close by. It definitely passed through a Russia mail-server. But that's as far as I got."

Vic did a half-jump in the lounge. "But that's great! Confirmation that it came from Russia, like the email said."

George let out a long sigh. "I wish it were that easy, Vic. Anyone can rent a relay server in Russia. Even now. Doesn't really prove anything. All it proves is that whoever sent it wanted it to go through Russia along the way."

Fatima twisted her legs down to the floor and rose up on her arms. "So, my husband. Inconclusive."

"Yes, wife. Inconclusive."

Fatima levered herself into a half-crouch. "Well, I'm grateful you tried. Although I am a bit with Vic on this. If it was a complete joke, they wouldn't have gone through the effort. Can't be that easy to rent a Russian mail server."

"T'ain't hard."

"Oh George, don't be such a wet blanket. You did well." Vic gave him a brief hug. "Come in, close the door. We may not have disproved anything, but one thing we do know–"

"Is that Dan is shady," Fatima cut in. "Which we knew before. Although it doesn't hurt to get a reminder, by way of Russia, or points..." She shrugged. "Points otherwise and elsewhere. Speaking of Russia, Vixen, and we should put on a pot of tea, he must be freezing in that t-shirt, by the way, nice one, Scorpions Crazy World tour, vintage, and we have the vinyl, you know the kids are getting back into the '80s in a big way. They also have a Russian connection, which is–"

It was Vic's turn to cut off her friend, "Spit it out, Fats. Speaking of Russia?"

"Yes, I was getting to that, calm down. I'm the one who's supposed to be twitchy. Or touchy. Emotional.

Whatever. Motor mouth plus baby hormones, you know. Fundamentally a bit upset."

"Right," said Victoria. "Russia."

"Russia. Sberbank. The people who were going to buy that other bank, the British one. George was looking into it. But it's probably a bit too soon to go wittering on about all that."

"Wittering on about what?" A strange voice called from the landing outside. "Fitsy? You receiving?"

"Oh, bloody hell, it's Francis." Fatima blushed darker than a postbox. She grabbed the throw pillow off the couch and plopped down, pillow over her belly like a shield. "WE'RE IN HERE, FRANKIE," she shouted. "COME UP, COME IN."

George mouthed 'her brother' apologetically at Vic. He bundled into the kitchen to boil the kettle himself. A man not much bigger than Fatima nudged open the door. Similar size, but a contrast in couture – Burberry coat, Prada man purse, Thomas Pink shirt with two buttons undone to signal casual Saturday morning. Almost afternoon, thought Vic.

She was closest. And Fatima seemed to have muted herself. Might as well help out. "Take your coat?"

"Yes, thanks." Francis shrugged off one shoulder and then stopped. "Have we met?"

Victoria held out a hand for the coat. "Victoria."

Francis stopped removing his coat. "Ah, yes! You're Fatima's friend. Something Christmas-y. Donner. Or. Blitzen. Wait..." He shrugged out of the other shoulder. "Vixen!"

"Only my closest friends call me that," said Vic, letting the coat slump to the floor.

Some fabric was too high-thread-count to flop. Francis handed the still slightly upright coat to her. "Perfect! Any friend of Fitsy is a friend of mine. Francis Lepic, by the way."

"Not Lapicki?" Vic gave him the side eye. "Are you sure you're related?"

"Yes, very sure, although I haven't used THAT name since before St. Peter's. Lepic is so much more...." Francis looked around the small lounge from which George had vanished. "Sophisticated." He saw the look on her face. "And we have met. It's certainly not that I think all Black people look alike."

Victoria turned to her friend on the couch. "Fitsy, dear? Is there a good place for your insufferable brother's coat?"

Fatima had covered her face with the pillow. "He's not insufferable," she said, voice muffled. "I suffer him all the time. Hall closet."

"I heard that," said Francis. "And I heard something else as well. What is too soon to be talking about?"

"I'm pffgled", mumbled Fatima through the throw pillow.

"Speak up, Fits," said Francis, plopping down on the couch next his sister. "And remove that hideous pillow."

Fatima lowered the pillow but kept a firm grasp. She stared straight ahead. "It's a lovely pillow. Oxfam."

"Of course it's Oxfam," interrupted Francis.

"Oh, pregnant, Frankie. I'm pregnant."

Francis leaped off the couch. "Pregnant? Fitsy, this is excellent. Fantastic news! You little devil." Francis did a cha-cha step in the small section of cleared floor. "First in the family to make a family. We should celebrate." He was stopped by the look on his sister's face. "Right. Can't do champagne. What a shame. And you will definitely have to slow down the adventures. Can't see you roaming Afghanistan in a Baby Bjorn." Francis paused reflectively. "Although you of all people could find one to match the burqa. Not that you've ever cared about matching. Have you told Mum and Dad?" Fatima favoured him with a stone face. He ploughed onward. "And where is that charming husband of yours?"

George came out of the kitchen with the tea set on a tray. "Cuppa tea?"

– § –

The little updates are always more disruptive than the big, mused Dan. Name of the firm, unchanged. Tasteful brass plate near the doorbell, exactly the same. And still open on Saturdays. But the doorbell was now one of those video camera smart things. And Sellen was no longer at the helm. No use fretting 'bout spoiled cheese, he thought. He pressed the fat round button below the camera.

"May I help you?" An accent meant to convey disdain. Dan chuckled. No way that lady grew up sounding like that. Same as I sounded different a few decades back. Better than a change of clothes, to change people's minds about you. But a bit harder to take off.

"Why ma'am, I sure hope so," replied Dan. "I'm here to see Josh, about a contract that'll be worth his while."

"Is Mr. DeVilliers expecting you?"

"Oh, see now, Josh's an old friend. He'll find a way to make himself...." What was that word? "Available."

"I'm afraid we haven't been introduced." If words were weather, conditions went from autumn to arctic. "Whom shall I say is calling?"

"Well now, no need to sound so snippy. Tell Josh it's Dan, from the bank. The Sberbank. With an S-B-E-R." Dan gave waved into the fisheye of the video bell. "Sber."

"One moment."

Josh's office, formerly Hugh's, was a bit warmer than the reception. "Let's reset," said Josh, standing in front of the imposing desk. "Mrs. Evans is very protective of my time. Fortunately for us both, I have a break in the schedule." Josh motioned with a folder to armchairs flanking the console table by the window. "But you and I are not old friends. Certainly, Sellen & Sellen can assist with contracts, but I am curious. What brings you to ask for me by name?"

Dan unbuttoned his leather duster. "Pardner, in case you can't tell, I'm from the great state of Texas." He took the far chair and spread his legs, pausing to brush the tail of his coat off one thigh. "In Texas, we're not much for jokin'. More of a put up or shut up kind of a place." Dan offered the other chair to Josh with a casual nod. "And this is a put up or shut up kind of a case."

Josh moved to the window but didn't sit. "Right now, sir, we have no case."

"Au con-trair-o, mi amigo," replied Dan. "Your partner Hugh and I tried to buy a bank. A British bank. With money from a Russian bank." Josh raised an involuntary hand of caution that Dan ignored. "Now, some might call that unpatriotic. Others might call it capitalism. I call it a deal that went south, 'cause my money's stuck. And we still don't have a bank."

– § –

Vic surveyed the sitting room. George had put the tea things on a folding tray. Fatima's colonization of the coffee table was not worth fighting – laptop, articles, slips of notes, a purse that was more properly a rucksack. "So," offered Vic, "to what do we owe this visit, Frankie?"

"I prefer Francis." He perched on the couch next to Fatima, a person-sized space between them on the small settee. "Only Fitsy calls me Frankie these days."

"Yes, what does bring you calling, Frankie?" Fatima rolled the r to emphasize the 'Frank'. "You could have just rung."

"True, I could have, but then I would have missed out on your big news." He made a round belly shape in the air. "And I also have big news."

Fatima put the pillow between herself and Francis. "Do tell, brother dear."

"Actually, it's more like news and a favour."

"Shocking," replied Fatima. "Although if I recall, the last time I tried to do you a favour, I nearly ended up in prison."

"Calm down, Fits. Overnight detention, not prison. Besides, it's not that kind of favour. I simply need you to hold off on reporting a story for a few days."

"What? Let someone else get a scoop?" Fatima snorted. "Are you daft? Not in my nature. What's the story?"

"I know. I know. But it's about me. Which is why I thought I'd come 'round personally. Here's the sitch." Francis paused to put his mug down in a less-cluttered corner of the coffee table. "Tomorrow, PR newswires will announce that I've been appointed Managing Director of Nomura Food & Beverage Investments Asia."

"Congratulations, Frankie. But that's not exactly my beat."

"Fair enough. But in MY part of the City, it IS big news when someone like me gets a new job–"

Fatima broke in. "Hence, the press releases, that I usually skip, because they're puff pieces about how Muzzlethwaite-Rodgers will be leveraging his, and it's almost always his, years of experience and financial acumen to create strategic synergy across pools of trans-national capital. Or other such nonsense. They all sound like they've been written by AI. Which they probably have been. Although if I see your name, I might actually search for meaning in the fog of corporate hot air."

"Exactly." Francis blew the ball dead with swinging arms. "You'll skim the releases, because you can't help yourself, and one will be my promotion announcement, and you'll notice that I'm moving to Singapore. Because that's where the fund is incorporated." Francis picked up a loose printout he'd knocked onto the floor by accident. "And I wanted to tell Mum and Dad in person, before you let the cat out of the handbag."

"Oh, Francis, that's the favour?" Fatima hit her brother with the throw pillow. "Singapore? 'Logistically supported', I assume?"

"Yes, yes. Full package. Flat, car, club membership, maid allowance, et cetera."

"Good for you. Probably bad for Nomura, and certainly bad for the world's carbon balance. But good for you." Fatima leaned over and gave him a half-hug. "When do you fly out?"

"Wednesday."

Vic searched her memory banks for the last time she had seen Fatima at a loss for words. Half-open mouth, nothing coming out of it. Looked quite cute, even with the faint spit-rainbow shimmer. Still, quite a novelty. Given his ability to cause that reaction, perhaps it was a pity Frankie was leaving town.

– § –

"I'm afraid I need you to explain again your business here. Mr. Sellen is on extended leave." Josh tapped his folder on the arm of the empty chair.

"On second thought," he continued, "perhaps it would be better to await his return and resume your dealings directly with Hugh."

"Cool your jets, pardner." Dan leaned back, hands in the wide pockets of his duster. "And I don't think Hugh's coming back to this ranch. When you rodeo with the folks we were dealing with, an extended vacay is one way. But no matter. Here's what you're wanting." Dan withdrew a USB key from his right hip pocket. He rolled it across his knuckles like a poker chip, gold contacts flashing in the office light. "This token allows us to access the Ethereum account. Which will make both of us happy." The USB key vanished inside Dan's meaty palm. "And very, very rich."

Josh covered his chin with one hand and walked slowly back to his desk. The soft carpet muffled his footsteps, making the huff of his breath the loudest sound in the room. Dan watched as Josh made a circuit of the desk, placing his folder on the blotter, just so, closing a drawer left infinitesimally open, straightening a pen. Josh sat down and sighed. "No," he said.

"No?" A quiet heat flickered in Dan's question.

"No," repeated Josh. "I don't think that's good enough. I have no proof that you engaged our firm while Hugh was in charge. And I have a duty of confidentiality, a duty of concern, to my clients."

"Clients? We were partners!" Dan rocketed out of the chair. He slapped the USB stick down on Josh's desk. "PROOF? This here lil' token will unlock the account, with the password that you have on file. How much more proof do ya need?"

Josh was unmoved. "That's exactly it. There are any number of ways that a security token could end up in the hands of a new owner. For all I know, you found it in a rubbish tip. Which is precisely why clients involved in these types of transactions are required to have both token AND password, passwords that, by the way, we do NOT keep on file." Josh nudged the USB drive back towards Dan with the edge of the folder. "Even if we did, I'll remind you that Sellen & Sellen is still on retainer to the lawful owner of the account, whoever that proves to be."

"Son, it proves to be Daniel Firestone, but it's plain I ain't gonna convince you right here and now." Dan pocketed the USB key and stomped back to the window. He looked out, hands in fists. "No matter. I'll come back with the password. Phillip'll have it, for sure." Dan turned, brushing his coat flat. "This ain't goodbye. It's not even 'so long'. I'll see you shortly, and then we'll do business." Dan bustled out in a slap of leather, his rough energy such that Josh failed to notice the burnt imprints of two boot heels in the carpet below the window.

CALL YOUR MOTHER

Having missed her chance at a posh life, Vic goes couch surfing

"Frankie," said Fatima, after what felt like a one-year vow of silence. "Won't be hard to keep your news under wraps. Wednesday is..."

"Yes, I know," replied Francis. He held up four fingers and counted them off. "The day after the day after the day after tomorrow." Francis pensively tapped a finger. "Sunday, I put my things from the flat in storage. Unless you want the espresso machine, that is. It's a La Marzocco.

"Monday, I clear out my current desk, secure office and all that, no entry on the weekends, especially for people being removed from the system. Hence why I won't see Mum and Dad until Tuesday, which is also the day I turn in the lease on the E-tron. Hopefully they'll give me a ride back to the hotel Nomura booked for me. Which is miles from Heathrow, even though I know for a fact that Swissair, or Swiss, Lufthansa, whoever they are now on code-share, fly to Singapore from City airport. Funny what they choose to economize on. You can be sure it's the kickbacks to the travel agency for brand loyalty that are costing us an extra twenty pound in car fare to Twickenham, but the ops managers don't see any of that." Vic observed that Fatima's brother could muster almost as impressive a words-per-minute rate as Fatima. She busied herself with her tea and tuned out until mention of food.

"So I thought, one, since I wouldn't be seeing you for a while, two, since you are doing me a favour in keeping M&D in the dark for an extra day, three, we have scrumptious news to celebrate in the form of a your growing-for-a-good-reason belly, I, your brother Francis, should be taking you and the father of your sprog out for dinner. We can even take your peng friend along, although she is a bit mouthy. I guess all the better for eating with."

"Francis." Fatima spoke up before Vic could register the insult. "Enough. I gave you a pass on the 'insufferable', but you have to stop doing this."

"Doing what?" asked Francis.

"This. Blithely disregard your sister AND her husband for months on end, then crash into our lives on no notice with big changes and big news, ask for a favour, casually throw money, hospitality, and unsolicited advice around as if that might make up for ignoring us almost since the wedding." It was Francis' turn to be gobsmacked.

"Which is not to say that it's not nice to see you," continued Fatima. "I'm genuinely glad for you. But if you really wanted to do us a favour in return, instead of dinner at one of your posh hangouts, I'd rather you looked something up for me. Let's not kid ourselves. Part of the reason why you don't call much is that George and I aren't exactly your genre. Shall we debate how unctuous was the amuse bouche? Besides, more than five minutes without mention of bank balances or upscale brands leaves you yawning. What was it last time we met, Goyard?"

"So last year," replied Francis, his composure returned. "Everyone knows Vuitton is back." He put a light hand on his sister's arm. "Look up what?"

"George?" Fatima asked. "Where did you get stuck?"

"Ahem." George cleared his throat. "Almost at the beginning. There's a bank. Or rather, enough crypto to buy a bank. Even after the latest crash. Sitting on the Ethereum ledger doing bugger all."

"Exactly," said Fatima. "And there would be a good story in it, if we had any idea why. Or better yet, who owns it."

"But it's crypto!" exclaimed Francis. "That's the point

of it. Anonymity. Nobody on the internet knows you're a dog. And it's between you and your dog what you do with your coins, your tokens, your NFTs, or your whatever-they-think-up-next."

"Public ledgers like Bitcoin and Ethereum lack privacy," said George. "It's easy to track transactions. But we don't have the inside nous to link addresses to institutions. Nomura probably does."

"It probably does," replied Francis, "but I can't ask the Coin Desk to track down some random number for my sister, now, can I?"

"Why not?" asked Fatima. "Tell them it's due diligence on a potential investor. The sums George looked at could buy up all the bars in Singapore. Even that silly one where the beer prices change by the hour."

"Ooh, Fitsy. You HAVE gotten around." Francis shrugged. "Fine. Why not, indeed. George, email me the deets. And sister dearest–"

"I know. We've got a home in Singapore. Or we will once you get there. So get there safely." Fatima gave him a proper hug. "All the best, Francis. Be nice to Mum and Dad. You know they don't like to drive much at night."

The departing swirl of Francis' Burberry took with it the energy of the day. Vic was wrung out. The afternoon sun ebbed in sympathy. George offered to cook, but Vic insisted she owed them takeout at least. Fatima accepted after a sly dig about Vic going to dinner with Francis instead. Vic didn't mind a bit of posh, but, Francis? Which is how Vic found herself back on the Broadway, heading towards a Thai restaurant. No way George would let their address go into an online delivery app.

Vic was grateful her freshly on phone rang on the way to, rather than on the way back. Fumbling around with hands full of wet restaurant bags, no thanks. She'd rather have a missed call. Although 'Unknown Caller' was not exactly compelling to pick up either.

"Hullo?" Curiosity killed the cat.

"Vicky!" Dan's voice filled her ear with twang, her stomach with dread. "How the heck are ya, Missy?"

"Dan," said Vic. "I'm outside. And a bit busy. What is it?"

"Now, filly, I don't need but a minute. How'd it go with the momma?"

Vic stopped on the broad pavement. "It didn't," she said.

"Tarnation, woman. I thought we talked about this," replied Dan.

Vic stepped under the awning of a drycleaners. "You talked about it. I haven't made up my mind."

"What's to make up? He's your only livin' kin, and I've a sure-fire plan to get him back on Earth in a way that won't trouble you none. But first, you have to trouble your momma. That's the whole damn point."

Vic stepped aside to allow a patron to enter. "Why are you so keen to bring Phillip back?"

"'Cause I know cowboys, and Phillip is surely one. Be easier to keep the Mexicans out of Texas than keep Phillip out of your funny little country. When he comes back, and it's a when, not if, I want it on MY terms. And if you had the sense God gave a horse, you would too. So, will you holler at your momma for me? Believe you me, it's the safest thing to do. For all our sakes. Keep me posted."

Vic held the dead phone to her ear for only a moment. The food will be getting cold, she thought. Much to discuss over dinner.

– § –

Josh spent the rest of Saturday searching Hugh's emails for any reference to Dan Firestone. A fruitless search, as it turned out, although in rereading the original correspondence, it was strangely plausible that the Russian money was originally from somewhere else. Quite why someone would want to launder US funds through a Russian bank was beyond his imagination. But imagination rarely billed by the hour. When email failed, Josh switched to Google. Here too, Dan Firestone was something of a shadow. The one reference Josh found was an obscure article about a failed crypto-currency exchange. An enterprising investigator appointed by the bankruptcy court had traced the bulk of the exchange's seed money to a small private equity firm in Texas. Cornudas Capital listed Daniel Firestone as Chairman and Chief Executive Officer in its Delaware articles of incorporation. No other mention. In Josh's still somewhat limited experience, it was no surprise that a company reached for comment on a failed investment might be a bit reticent. What was surprising was the magnitude of the failure. All of the assets, coins, tokens, and whatnot held by the exchange that had not become worthless overnight had been pledged as security for a swathe of unrepayable loans. This was a rare case where the exchange's investors had less than nothing. The portfolio of bad debts exceeded even the most optimistic swings of the crypto market.

Bad debts reminded Josh how much he loved his wife. Made easier now that the downturn in crypto currency had muted her talk of 'we would have been better off in Bitcoin', instead of the firm. That they now had spare cash to invest was precisely because he had done the opposite. With her help and blessing, she reminded. He had held her off at the time by telling her he would buy Bitcoin the moment anyone explained to him what application it had that was better than solid British pounds. Thanks to Cornudas Capital, he finally had his answer. Hard to trade, hard to value, hard to explain to the average client. But if you wanted to turn a very large sum of money into something close to zero, it was excellent.

– § –

The muted normalcy of George and Fatima's domestic routine gave Vic unusual peace. Not because she and Mal had been domestic. When he was working, he was usually gone before she woke up. Depending on how late she found inspiration, he was often asleep when she returned from the studio. She used to joke that they were lunch time lovers. Shift over, he'd return to the house around noon with fresh bread. More than enough incentive to start her workday from home. Some light sketching, clearing email, ordering materials in the quiet of the morning, late breakfast or early lunch with Mallory, then off to Spike Island. She was quite content to leave Mal with the washing up.

The sounds of dishes in the sink were all from her father. In hindsight, she hadn't been easy on him. A widowed single father, or so she thought for most of her life, he'd been stuck with somewhat of a wild child. Especially vivid was the washing up after yet another visit to Casualty. She'd removed the wing mirror from a Vauxhall Viva with her elbow, trying to overtake on the hard shoulder. She'd managed to keep the bike rubber side down, but her right arm was no good for further riding. The Vauxhall driver, having completed their own right turn, kept going. Perhaps they hadn't seen her bleeding. Her father joked that you'd have needed a wing mirror for that.

This was before she'd had her own cell phone, so she'd had to limp to the nearest pub to call home. The pub's lav tissues were the almost plastic-coated kind. Did nothing to clean up the cut, smeared the blood around more than anything else. But that wasn't the worst of it. She'd invented a tale that didn't involve two wheels or her own fault, but her father had spotted the little red-and-white Yamaha on his way in. Hard to put one over the old man. Very old man. It was two full moons after she healed up before she found where he'd hidden the key. A key he'd forced from her as the price of his taxi service to St. Peter's Hospital.

Later, her arm properly bandaged and the bloodied handkerchief she'd borrowed from him in the rubbish, he'd cooked a simple dinner, pasta with tuna, sauce from a jar. Something she could eat with one hand, since staining her shirt was no longer an issue. They'd hardly spoken during dinner. That wasn't unusual, although Vic could feel thicker than usual gusts of disappointment wafting from his shoulders and head, coalescing under the rafters in a cloud of funk. She had offered to clear the table on one wing, which he wouldn't hear.

"Life is long, Victoria," he'd said. "Full of events you think you'll remember. Like the birth of your daughter, or this trip to Casualty sixteen years later. But you don't, Vic. You forget. You forget what clothes you were wearing, what you had for supper. Sure, you remember the hospital, but not the boring bits, the waiting to be seen, the going over the discharge instructions. Just the highlights, the stitches, perhaps the business where they made me push you out in a wheelchair despite knowing you could walk perfectly well. But most of it, you'll forget. You'll forget this dinner, you'll forget having done the washing up, you'll forget most of the times I woke you for school, certainly half of what you learn there. Even if you try to polish it over in your mind, the noise of countless tomorrows will swamp our memories of the past. And you'll find yourself wondering, what was it your father told you, after this particular misadventure? You'll wonder, what lecture did he give? What profound life advice did I receive, so tantalizingly close to retrieval from my rotten memory banks? But you'll forget. Which is good, because it means you didn't get killed. So you sit and think about what you want to remember from today while I do the dishes."

In a way, he wasn't wrong. She hadn't thought about that night in years. Yet she could still taste the tinned tuna in her mouth, feel the surgical tape of the gauze pad tugging at her arm, its white padding incongruous against her ruined t-shirt and skin. Why it was this evening that this memory found her, she wasn't sure. Perhaps it was the change of scene.

Like most designers, Vic found sleep sofas a necessary evil. George and Fatima's was the kind where the bench shifts over and the back folds down. Preferable to the thin mattresses that unfold from beneath the cushions, but still something less than a proper bed. And for all that, she was at ease, tucked under the spare sheets in the living room.

She should be trying to talk to Lilith right now, she thought, instead of casually eavesdropping on her friends. But how? Focus on 'Hiya, mum' as she fell asleep? Honestly, she'd rather think about anything other than her mother. Except perhaps why she hadn't mentioned Dan's second call to Fatima and George. Dan's impatience would make them even more suspicious of his motives. I'm suspicious of his motives, she thought. But talking through scenarios with F-n-G might box her in. The best thing to do was stay out of it completely. Let Dan deal with Dan's problems. Stick to diving for Mal, making a few sticks, and pretending she was a proper orphan rather than an abandoned child. Scratch that. Abandoned adult businesswoman, with a brother, disgusting gobshite killer though he may be. And a mother, a hateful one, but the only way back to the truth of her father.

Vic gathered the duvet with one hand and rolled over. It was all so much simpler underwater. Sure, Thames visibility varied from truly awful to mild silt. Even on the sunniest days, things beyond a few feet were lost in a dusty brown glow. But there were almost always a few fish. Dozens of bottles, some shreds of plastic bags. Fragments of terra cotta brick, shoulders rounded, reds and browns richer and more vibrant the older they were. The gentle ebb and bob of the currents, the quiet blanket of water disturbed only by the bubbles from her regulator. It was shockingly peaceful under the river, in the heart of the city. And despite being only a few yards from the bustle of the CBD, you don't meet anyone by chance underwater. Definitely not your long-lost mother. The familiar calm slowed her breathing – the more she dived, the less air she used up.

In her mind's eye, she retraced the last search square, square more euphemism than method of organization.

The bed of the river was dynamic, snags and snarls appearing and disappearing with each storm surge, sometimes for no reason at all. There had been something bottle shaped at the corner of her vision. Along the bed of the Thames, Vic reminded herself, there was always something bottle shaped. Plastic bottle shaped, mostly. What nagged at her was the flash of black and gold. In her half-forgotten memory, it looked like a black anemone, haloed by green stringers of weed. Weren't anemones supposed to live in the tropics? Black and gold tentacles screamed poison. She discovered she was dreaming when it spoke. "Victoria, take that idiotic thing out of your mouth," it said. "You don't need that here."

Vic responded with a bloop of startled bubbles. A tentacle elongated from the gelatinous foot of the anemone. She batted it away with a neoprene glove, but it wrapped around her wrist and pulled her in. The strength of that writhing mess was enormous. Or something had gone wrong with perspective. What had seemed a small polyp, at first glance the size of her fist, was now wide enough to swallow her whole body. Vic closed her eyes as the tentacle drew her into its open mouth.

"Hello, daughter." Lilith stood at the far end of a white conference table in a somber executive ensemble of low heels, charcoal trouser suit, and white silk blouse. Vic sat, unceremoniously dumped and dripping, in the Herman Miller office chair at the other end. Her bathing suit rucked against the mesh seat. She had been dispossessed of dry suit, tank, and scuba gear. Dry clothes, on the other hand? Not so important.

"Hiya, mum." Younger Vic would have cursed her lack of repartee. I guess the current me is more functional, she thought. Certainly less prone to beating herself up about missed opportunities. "Wicked suit, mum. Conference room's a bit WeWork, though. What's going on?"

"You tell me, Victoria. You were the one who called."

DOMESTICITY

George makes a promise, Vic goes for a drive,
Francis burns a bridge

"George, my love, can you please close the door when you pee?" Fatima was on her back on top of the covers. "Vic's downstairs."

"She's fast asleep. And we're married," replied George.

"All true. But that doesn't mean I want to listen to your wee tinkling around the bowl." George grunted and flushed the toilet. Fatima held her tongue through running taps and teeth brushing noises, door still open.

George returned, a small fleck of toothpaste on the right side of his lower lip. He took in the still fully dressed form of his wife on the bed. "Oy, what's this? What have you been thinking about?" he asked. "Because if it's Spurs, they've got no chance again this year. Forever fourth. At best."

Fatima had to laugh. Her lack of interest in football was legendary. Which aligned well with George, despite that every British Y-chromosome included vestigial genes for tracking the footie. She levered herself upright with both hands, the weight of their progeny already changing how she shifted from one position to another. "Come here, Georgie." She kissed away the speck of froth. "Mm, minty."

"No, seriously, what are you thinking about?" he repeated. "I know that look."

"The law firm. Sellen & Sellen." Fatima put her hand over George's on the bed covers.

"What about them?"

"Vic told me once that they were part of the whole Sberbank affair. I think she said 'implicated'. 'Fucking well implicated.'"

"That sounds like Vic."

"So I did a little digging, as one does, and it seems the former head of the firm is on indefinite leave." Fatima gave George's hand a squeeze. "Which sounds to me a bit like permanent vacation, also known as…"

George finished the thought, "…not alive." He gently disentangled his fingers from hers. "This is what you think about while I'm getting ready for bed?"

"Some nights, yeah. It's not like my brain stops working at sundown."

"Well, mine has. It's been an odd Saturday. Vic arrives at the crack of dawn. I spend half the morning in the van, chasing emails. Then your brother shows up. When was the last time we saw him?"

"The wedding. And that was only because Mum made him come."

"Right," said George. "How you two come from the same family–"

"–is as simple as sending the son off to a public boarding school, and the daughter to comprehensive. Frankly, I think I got the better end of the deal. I mean, Singapore? All you can do is eat and shop, and poor Francis is uninterested in the taste of his food. He's all about the presentation."

"I believe he likes to shop."

"There is that," replied Fatima. She picked up his hand again and guided it to the bottom of her jumper. "Will you look into Sellen & Sellen for me? What happened to Hugh, and whatnot? Because, you know, sex during pregnancy is perfectly safe."

"Yes, I read that on the Internet," said George, kissing her once. "Which means it must be true. But tomorrow, after we get to Birmingham, ok?"

"Tomorrow, Sellen?" clarified Fatima.

"Yes, Sellen tomorrow. We can do the other thing right now."

– § –

Vic pushed the office chair back from the conference table and stood. At least Mother put me in a one-piece, she thought. Didn't solve the wet-backside-on-mesh problem, but with all the diving, she was used to that. She stood, which helped tremendously. "I suppose I did call you. To warn you. Dan has been begging me to talk to you–"

"That tedious man," said Lilith, leaning in, hands planted on the table.

"Agreed. I don't want to talk to him either." Vic continued before her mother could interrupt again. "He has some scheme to bring Phillip back to my part of the world. I'm worried Phillip might be tempted."

"Worried?" asked Lilith.

"Yeah, worried. I think Dan wants to kill him."

"So do I," said Lilith. "But it will be hard to stop him."

"Which him?"

"Oh, either of them. Dan knows he's no match for me here. I'm equally limited in your world. And as for your brother? I've told him that he needs to be patient. But he is a child. A naïve child."

"A killer child. Not quite so innocent as you make him out to be."

"Inexperienced in the ways of the world. The current controversy will be buried and gone in a decade or three.

Random bombings in London won't even make the history books of 2075. Phillip thinks his only moment is now. Perspective!" Lilith shook her head. "So hard to achieve." Lilith waved her hand and the conference room fell away.

A blast of air sucked the remaining moisture from Victoria's hair, giving her a chill. She and her mother were side-by-side in an antiquated roadster, Lilith nonchalant at the wheel. A country lane dipped and curved beneath them at Formula One speed, hedgerows alternating with stubbled fields. The road wriggled past its boundary markers in a distinctly non-linear way, paved homage to horse tracks, forgotten landmarks and long dried streams. Lilith hugged the racing line, swerving and bouncing the car by reflex. They swooped under a green tunnel of overhanging trees. Branches whipped by short inches from the open top.

"MOM," Victoria shouted over the wind. A Jaguar SUV topped the rise above them, occupying equal majority of the road. Seemed to match their velocity as well, but in the 'head on collision' direction.

"MOM!" The road widened. The wall of trees on the left retreated by a yard. The Jaguar flashed by their wheels, lane snapping to its original geometry in their wake.

"ISN'T IT FABULOUS?" asked Lilith. "I DO ALL MY SERIOUS THINKING WHILE DRIVING." A wink of sunlight reflected in her round glass goggles.

"HARD TO TALK," shouted Victoria, thankful for the cushion of a thick tweed jacket beneath the shoulder belt. She glanced down. Trousers and a pair of quite marvelous boots. At least the wardrobe had improved.

Lilith braked hard, cutting a sharp turn into an open field. Mud peened the wheel arches like a snare drum. They bounced a slow oval around the perimeter of the field. "How's this?" asked Lilith, slewing the car to avoid a stump.

"Still quite uncomfortable," said Vic. "Can we get something better than a tractor suspension? Or perhaps even stop?"

"Tractor?" Lilith pushed up her goggles. "Au contraire, daughter of mine. This is a very modern Morgan. BMW inline six. I do TRY to keep up." Lilith slipped the gearshift into neutral with an elegant finger and let the divots of the field bring the car to a halt. She turned to her daughter. "Daniel. The problem of Daniel."

Vic unfastened her seatbelt and loosened her cramped shoulders. "The problem is Phillip."

"I beg your pardon," said Lilith, her lips a tight line.

"Hear me out, Mum. You said that Phillip's problems go away if he can wait them out. But we both know he can't. Won't. Whatever." Vic gave a helpless shrug. "Daniel wants something. I don't know what. But if we can figure that out, perhaps we have a chance of resolving this."

Lilith removed her goggles, giving Vic a study of the flecks of gold in her otherwise black irises. Lilith put her hand back on the shifter. "You don't live this long by leaving things to chance. The only thing to do is to convince Phillip to be more patient."

"Which you just told me you can't do."

"No, I said it would be hard. Which is different from impossible. And unfortunate, because here, impossible things are highly achievable."

"Fine. Do what you want. You always do." Vic shoved open the car door. "What should I tell Dan?"

"Tell him you couldn't reach me. I firmly intend to ignore you until I know more."

"And if I find something out, and need to reach you?"

"Assemble your friends at the points of the star. A strong call, I will attend."

Vic wanted to say more, but the car was gone. So was the muddy field. She was cold and awake in the dark, on the fold-out bed in Fatima's apartment, duvet rucked at her feet.

When Fatima came down, Vic was dressed and sitting

on a reconstituted sofa. She'd stacked the folded sheets neatly on the other seat.

"Talked to Mum last night," said Vic.

"Ah." A slow nod from Fatima. "Fancy a cup of tea?"

"Good Lord, yes." Vic rose from the couch. "But let me fix it. You're getting as big as a whale."

"A small-boned, highly capable whale." Fatima laughed. "A pygmy whale. Perhaps a dwarf sperm whale, know what I mean?"

Vic smiled in return. "That's terrible. A killer is what you are. Killer whale."

Fatima raised both arms in triumph. "Orca. Queen of the seas. Although I think orcas are technically dolphins."

Victoria opened various cabinets in the small kitchen. "Where do you hide the tea?"

"Porcelain jar by the toaster," replied Fatima. "But you're avoiding the obvious. How'd it go with Mumsy?"

"About the same. Still arrogant as hell. Still convinced of her own genius."

"She does have more experience than the two of us put together," countered Fatima.

"Yeah, but it's hundreds of years of the same ideas, over and over. It's like she hasn't learned any of the right things."

"Such as?" asked Fatima, taking the electric kettle

from Vic and filling it from the tap. Fatima put the kettle back on its round base and nodded her chin meaningfully at the outlet.

Vic switched on the wall socket. They watched the kettle in silence for a moment, waiting for the rumble of water vaporising on the hot plate inside. Vic turned to her friend. "Like dealing with young people. Phillip, in particular." Vic reopened the cabinet where she had glimpsed mugs and took down two. "She thinks she can convince him not to do anything rash."

Vic considered the mugs and handed Fatima the Little Mermaid. "In keeping with the ocean theme," she said, inspecting 'British Telecommunications PLC – Celebrating 30 Years of Private Ownership' for dust. "But she hasn't been young for those same hundreds of years. Or properly been around young people. Phillip is going to do whatever he wants. I know it. Daniel knows it. And Dan wants Phillip to come back, for some reason. He's going to use him for something."

"Wait," said Fatima. "Who's using who? And for what?"

"I don't know." The kettle switched off, startling them both. "But I don't trust Dan. If Phillip comes back now, I feel it's going to…"

"Going to what?" asked Fatima.

"End," said Vic. "Badly."

– § –

Francis considered the mound of bubble wrap and flatpack in the corner for the umpteenth time. It will have to get done today, old chap. Doesn't mean it has to get done now. The van was set to arrive at half four. He glanced at his Longines. Five hours. He'd hardly need three. And rather than start things off badly with Nomura, why not use his last day with an HSBC laptop to do some sleuthing? He hadn't the heart to tell his sister that the move to Singapore was motivated in part by the closing of HSBC's Canary Wharf office. They were going to send him to Birmingham. Cheaper to hire FinTech programmers there. But who wants to go to Birmingham? Other than his sister's husband, of course. Nice fellow, if a bit gormless. Apparently fertile, although the thought of his little sister shagging was...well, certainly wasn't the first time.

He inserted his not-quite-expired employee smartcard into the laptop and logged in. Yet another reason to hop over to Nomura. HSBC had its head in the sand when it came to crypto. One wee trading desk in Hong Kong. But it did have access to SWIFT's KYC registry. Share your Know Your Customer data, receive it back from counterparties. Which in HSBC's case was every exchange in the world. Francis brought up George's emailed list of transactions on his phone. All well over the reporting threshold. Careless, he thought, although the boys moving to Birmingham had long worked out algorithms to cross-correlate suspicious small buys. What about withdrawals? Any matching funds transfers in the history? Searching beyond a narrow window was going to get him in trouble, but what were they going to do, dismiss him? He scrolled the email with a finger. Depending on the source of funds, clearing would take between one and three days. Francis typed in a date four days before the first deposit. A long list. Unsurprising. Capital is going to flow. He opened a second window and keypunched a date range for the second deposit. As long. At this rate, he'd be better off packing. He flipped idly between the two windows. LoneStar TumbleCoin. What on earth was that?

DATE NIGHT

Vic takes off, Rahim gets frisky, Fatima gets worried

"Well, Vixen, good news is, you're probably not in any immediate danger." Fatima carried their mugs into the kitchen. "I mean, you can stay as long as you like."

"No, I get it. Dan needs me too much to do anything nefarious. Lilith is working on Phillip. And you two have a dinner date in Birmingham."

"You make it sound so...transactional," replied Fatima. "You could wish me luck, you know."

"I do wish you luck, Fats, but you don't need it. I'm sure Dot will be over the moon at your news. I just feel a little..."

"Lost? Adrift? Confused? Angry I won't shut up?"

"Too late for that," said Vic. "I think I'm lonely."

"Oh, Vixen, why wouldn't you be? Two years searching for Mal." Fatima gave her a one-armed hug. "Why don't you give your new friend a call. What was his name?"

"Fabio."

Fatima giggled. "Classic."

"What?" asked Vic. "It's a name."

"Yes, I know. Listen, I need to put on some proper clothes. George will no doubt be impatient to leave. But you really are welcome to stay. Seriously."

Victoria went into the living room and zipped up her overnight bag. "Dan called me yesterday," she said. "Wanted to know how I was getting on with Mum."

Fatima stopped on the stairs. "When was this?"

"When I went out for the Thai."

"And?"

"And I told him I hadn't made up my mind."

"But you talked to Lilith last night!"

"Well, yes," replied Vic. "But that wasn't exactly planned. And I got a big naff off, didn't I? She said something like 'tell him you couldn't get through', as if she was some kind of switchboard operator."

"For Hell's phone exchange. So now what?"

"I think I'll go home. Dan can wait, and despite all the aggro, I believe Lilith would let me know if Phillip came back. Somehow. Besides, I've got furniture to make. A business to run. The customers don't serve themselves."

"Fatima," George called down the stairs, "it's getting to be time to go."

"I know," she replied. "But come down and say

goodbye to Vic. She's leaving."

"What, now? I've got to polish my shoes."

"It's all right," replied Fatima. "I think she's seen you in your stocking feet before."

Victoria was depressingly familiar with the forecourt of the Newbury Central KFC. Newbury had the most reliable charging stations of all places about halfway between London and Bristol. She had given up on Tescos. Too many shoppers with Teslas. But there was only so much Kentucky Fried she could stomach. The vegan burger wasn't terrible, but each time she ordered one she heard her father's voice asking, "Burgers? Sure, I like them. But do you eat them before food, or after?"

She scrolled through her email on the phone, cursing once again her decision to get the smaller screen. The idea was that she'd spend less time on it if it were harder to read. She spent as much time, and her eyes hurt. Hoisted on her phone petard. At least it had an app that told her when the EV had enough charge to get home.

Vic's thoughts wandered to the red leather jacket on the passenger seat, and to the lilac business card tucked inside it. Was the colour choice confidence, or an echo of the girl he'd left behind? Perhaps Fabio just liked Prince. Vic liked Prince. And Janelle Monae. Which didn't mean she necessarily wanted to sleep with a woman again, but a phone call wouldn't hurt. Or a text. Text is better. Something low key. 'Takeout coffee by the Arnolfini? Leave the large men behind. -Vic'. Her phone pinged immediately. It was only the van telling her it was time to go home.

Vic spent a quiet Sunday night alone in the house. Checking the phone too often, but otherwise quiet. She had toyed with the idea of going to work. She wanted to talk to Rahim, but not urgently enough to disturb him on the weekend. Disturbed was the right word. She recalled the last Sunday they had been in the studio together. Rahim had called, not pleading exactly, but Vic could tell he needed someone to talk to, and an excuse to get away. He showed up so stressed he was shaking. His family had decided he needed an arranged marriage. She'd idly suggested they smoke some bud. He'd surprised her by agreeing.

"There is no injunction against hashish in the Koran," he'd said.

"This isn't hashish, Ree. It's Mary Jane," she'd replied. "You shouldn't be smoking."

With each long exhale, they'd chant "Bad. For. Health." until they got the giggles. A strong case of them, stash quality control these days desperately uncertain. But it was also the vibe. With a strait-laced noob like

Rahim, she needed a lot less to get...what was it exactly? Not high. Mellow. The edge of the 21st century panic taken off.

Afterwards, he'd managed to convince his father to give him more time to find a love marriage. That clock was ticking louder. They both heard it, at odd times, but didn't discuss it. The good part was that since then, they'd unwind with a joint on the occasional evening.

She never smoked up at home. Another legacy of her father, having sniffed once in her room and locked up her art supplies. When she'd worked up the nerve later to ask how he'd known, he'd told her that they had a familiarisation course for all single parents down at the Community Centre. He was a much better liar than she - more practice.

Monday, she woke oddly refreshed. So what, if Fabio hadn't texted her back. The van had a full charge, the firm had a backlog of orders, pandemic was over. Better yet, she was no longer in imminent threat of being eaten by a ghoul in the night. She called Fatima on the drive to the studio. "How did it go with Dot? All well?"

"Yes...and no." A rare pause from Fatima. "As predicted, she's delighted about the heir. Not so receptive to my plans for grandmotherly child-rearing. Surprisingly firm, in fact." Fatima imitated her mother-in-law. "Oh, it'd be lovely to see you all on the weekend. But of course, I'm too old now to be raising children. One on my own was quite enough." Fatima coughed, continuing in her normal voice. "I can see where George gets it from. Comes across a little soft, but there's real mettle underneath in there."

"Patience, Fats," said Vic. "Once George the Second appears, all bets are off."

"I was thinking Hussain. He is the son of Fatima, after all."

"Spoken like someone who won't be wanting help from Dorothy."

"Yeah," sighed Fatima. "It's complicated. Families. Even pint-sized ones like mine. Speaking of which, I heard from my brother."

"That was fast," said Vic.

"Yeah, I know, right? Seems he got into a bit of trouble this morning when he went to turn in his laptop. Accused of trying to steal clients. The phrase he gave me was 'over-careful scrutiny of a departing employee's activity'. He'd done a search where he shouldn't have, on the dates we'd given him. A search that turned up a number of sensitive transactions. HSBC said they were going to name him in a suspicious activity report to UK Financial Intelligence. Put a blight on his new job before it even began."

"Why didn't he say he was doing a favour for his sister?" asked Vic.

"Oh, Francis would never do that," said Fatima. "First of all, it would be an admission of wrongdoing. Besides, he has a self-interested image to maintain. That said, he is SLIGHTLY protective of me. Distant. Opposite. But protective.

"He brazened it out, said he was checking to ensure he hadn't left any land mines for his successor. I think what saved him is that George's dates led to a large sum linked to a debtor previously classified as insolvent. Frankie tried to argue for a bonus. They gave him a cardboard box. Told him to finish clearing out his desk."

"Who was the debtor?" asked Vic.

"LoneStar Tumblecoin."

"Sounds suspiciously American."

"It does, because it is. Backed by a private firm from Cornudas, Texas."

"Dan."

"Exactly. Full of shit, AND, full of crypto, which is curious, since HSBC thought he was skint."

– § –

There were days the giant desk he inherited from Hugh was the most glorious command post in the world.

There were other days when it felt like a millstone. Josh didn't mind payroll, paying bills. One must spend money to make money. What he hated was ambiguity, requests full of vagueness, misdirection when he wanted clarity. Hugh had warned him that most clients wanted more than what they asked for. Family members frozen out of joint assets, usually. "We're exploring selling the family firm. Could you take a look at the covenants? Simply exploring." The Sberbank business was equally maddening. There WAS a note in the meagre file from Hugh mentioning Dan Firestone. But not enough to prove the bona fides of Saturday's infuriating cowboy.

Josh kept returning to that awful email Hugh had sent, one of the last Hugh had written, to someone named Victoria. Josh had been in Westminster the day of the vote. And so had she, as evidenced by the news archive. 'Cardiff Woman Rides Motorcycle Into Thames'. Hugh clearly had been concerned that she'd interfere. How much did this rider know about the Sberbank scheme? Time he found out.

– § –

Rahim was hard at it when Vic reached, finishing another rod and gun case. "Did you pick up the acetone?" he asked.

"Oh, fuck," replied Vic. "Although 'hello' would have been a bit more inviting."

"You forgot the acetone."

"Ree, the weekend got a bit hectic. Had to drive to London and see Fatima. She's having a baby."

"That's what married people do, Ms. Vic. I'll get the acetone at lunchtime, if you tell me where you parked the van."

The morning passed. Vic returned a few calls and fiddled with sketches, occasionally helping Rahim with the glass in the doors. She was glad Rahim had gone out when the phone rang. Vic didn't like being observed on the phone. How anyone could walk down the street with it on speakerphone, she hadn't a clue.

"Victoria, I am sooo sorry." Fabio's voice was unmistakable, even if she had saved his number in contacts.

"Right," she replied.

"No, seriously. I didn't see your text until way late. Didn't want to ping and wake you."

"I'm a night owl."

"Oh, good," said Fabio. "Me too. But there was good reason. We had to go to a Strong Man event in Wigan, sign an endorsement contract. Why they couldn't do it over email, I really don't know." Theatrical sigh over the phone. "The event organisers make you put your phone in a lead bag, so there's no signal. Don't want footage leaking over social media. I tried explaining to them, footage all over social media IS the point."

"Mmm," said Vic again.

"Let me make it up to you. Dinner tomorrow?"

"Fine," said Vic. "Pick me up at The White Hart."

"The White Hart?" replied Fabio. "We can do better than that for dinner."

"Don't worry. You will."

In the afternoon, things got hairy at the studio. Rahim was on some kick about AI taking over the world. "They're going to automate everything, Ms. Vic. Soon, you'll ask your phone for a Danish stool, or a walnut sleigh bed, and a robot will carve it out for you. We've got five years. Ten, tops."

"In which case, Rahim, why are you here?"

Rahim grinned. "It beats the front desk. And I like the feel of creating something. Really making something." Rahim pointed at the laptop in the corner. "But those things are coming for us. Ten years."

"I don't see it, Ree. In ten years, we'll all be using computer-controlled saws, and clients will be sending us ever more impractical designs. But we'll still be working. We'll just be working with AI. It's like the Knowledge. You might not need to have all the roads of London memorised, but you still need to know how to drive. And talk to customers. The London black cab remains on the road."

"Perhaps, Ms. Vic. I think that's a rosy view."

Vic put down her drill. "Furniture, Rahim. It's heavy. Hard to ship from China."

"Malaysia," replied Rahim.

"Wherever. The posh types who buy Victoria Ali WANT it handmade."

"I know. But we make almost as much on Modern Legends. Have you thought about setting up a unit?"

"Is that what this is about?" asked Vic. "Expansion plans? Didn't you just say we'll be out of business in ten years?"

"Perhaps. We can make a lot of money in ten years."

Vic glanced at the patch of sky visible through the strip of window. Sunny. Which is NOT how she was feeling about this conversation. "Hold the fort, Rahim. I'm going for a pie. Want one?"

"No thanks, Ms. Vic. I don't think stray cat is halal."

"Very funny, Rahim. About as funny as your other idea. We'll talk about it later."

Vic liked to cut over to Brunel Square and walk along the water. She'd count the masts docked along Hanover Quay and pick in her mind which boat would be hers.

Like that light-blue one. Not too big to be unaffordable. Big enough to have a lav on board.

Mal, being tall, disliked sailboats. Vic thought there was something romantic about gliding along without a motor. Normally it was she who had to be drawn into conversation, Mal muttering about something random most hours of the day. But this was one game where he wouldn't play along. Best two days of a boat-owners life and all that. She'd remind him that "hole in the water you throw money into" was cliché. He'd reply that clichés were embodied wisdom. We repeat them because they held a germ of truth. Which was more truth than he often held, thought Vic. She could hold him right now.

Her feet took her to the pie shop on autopilot. There was a fancier bakery a few minutes further walk, but the smell of their bread was too similar to Mal's. Pulled her down dark paths, like the throw her father had once said was a favourite of her mother. Its only scent was the Tesco fabric softener, but that didn't stop her wondering how its owner must have smelled, or if she and mum had ever curled together in its warmth.

She could have stayed in the building. The studio had a nice café in the ground floor, but one flight of stairs wasn't enough to clear the mind. Besides, she liked the taste of this one's pie crust. It even had buttery in the name. Which gave her super greasy fingers when the phone rang, damn it.

"How was your date?" Fatima's voice was bright.

"It's tomorrow. And not really a date," replied Vic. "He's a friend."

"Hmph," snorted Fatima. "You're STILL too young for platonic friendship. He's clearly interested. Are you?"

"It's complicated."

"Right," said Fatima. "Let's simplify. Does he only talk about himself?"

"No, not really." Vic scratched at her nose. "He asked me about hobbies. I was going to tell him I like to dive in the Thames."

"Oh, God, PLEASE don't tell me you're going to spend the whole night going on about Mal."

"Have a little faith, Fats." Vic walked over to the railroad track side for some privacy. "I'm sure there will be lots to talk about. The boat club. You know, the sporting aspect. He's kind of a sports agent. And a DJ."

"A DJ?" Fatima scoffed.

"Yes, a DJ. He's opening for Paris Hilton in Ibiza."

"Opening for Paris Hilton," repeated Fatima. "Is that like when you had coffee with Colin Firth?"

"Probably. I googled him when I got home. There are at least five sets between him and Paris, but he IS opening. And I'll have you know that Colin and I shared a significant moment at the creamer station. He was aware of my presence."

"Yeah, because unlike the rest of the screamers at the autogrille, you didn't ask for a selfie. I still wouldn't exactly call that 'coffee with Colin'."

"Why not? It's technically correct. We had coffee, in the same café."

"Fine. But before you go running off to Ibiza, did you decide what to do about Dan?"

"Can't I just wait? Why do I have to decide at all?"

"Oh, Vix, you're the centre of it all. Obviously."

"Fair enough. But it's a moot point, anyway. Dan asked to meet."

"Really? Where? When?"

"Thursday. London Eye. Booked us a private pod, at 5pm. Sent me a QR code via text."

"That's a bit presumptuous."

"That's Dan. Expensive way to get me alone."

"Especially since he's bankrupt," said Fatima. "You want me to tag along?"

"Thanks, Fats, but I don't think so. I fancied a dive beforehand. And it's only the one ticket. He clearly wants a private audience. I'll be all right."

"But call me afterward."

"Immediately. Or 5:35-ish. I might have to pee.

Fairground rides do bad things to my system. By the way..."

"Yes?" asked Fatima.

"I got the strangest email," replied Vic.

"Stranger than the email from our dead Roman?"

"Almost. Do you remember that law firm, Sellen & Sellen?"

"Bollocks," Fatima spluttered. "Remember? I asked George to look into them."

"Did he find anything?"

"Not yet, other than the fact that Hugh Sellen is missing, most likely dead."

"Yes, besides that," said Vic. "About Josh DeVilliers."

"No idea. Who's Josh?"

"The new managing partner. He wrote me, asking about Sberbank. Wanted to know if I wanted to talk. And if I had the password."

"Password? That's odd," said Fatima.

"Extremely. Let me know if George finds anything."

"I will, Vixen. But in the meantime, stay safe. Feels like things are coming to a head."

"I know, Fats, I know. A head about to be removed from its neck."

FERRIS WHEEL BLUES

George draws a blank, Vic gets tilted

Vic bustled into the studio on Wednesday a little after 3pm. Not super uncommon – owner shifts are flexible, and more than a few nights she'd work through to the other 3 o'clock. Uncommon outfit, though, smart white dress under the leather jacket, a bit short for the weather. She did desultory paperwork for a few hours while Rahim worked at his bench. Finally, he lost patience and interrupted her work-as-work-avoidance.

"Is that makeup?" he asked. "Going out tonight?"

"Yeah. Meeting a friend."

"I hope not too soon." Rahim waved at two half-built cabinets bristling with wedges. "We've got work piled up."

"About that," said Vic. "I need to go to London tomorrow. Probably be gone all day."

"Which is why we need to expand. You and I together can't meet demand. And if you're out tonight and all day tomorrow, we'll only get further behind."

"Ree, I said I'd think about it." Vic stood and surveyed their work in progress, hands on hips. "This meeting tomorrow is really important. I'm a bit nervous about it. Which is why I called Fabio." She tapped one of the wedges with a painted fingernail. "If I try to do serious work this evening, I'll only break something."

"I don't get it, Ms. Vic," said Rahim. "You're normally so…" He trailed off.

"So?" asked Vic.

"Diligent. Like you lose yourself in the work. I can't count the number of times I've found you after an all-nighter. On weeks when we haven't been this busy. What's going on?"

"Rahim, you remember when that mad Texan came, and we stood in that circle."

"Yes. How could I not? That was an unusual day."

"Well, he's back."

"Your older gentleman? The one you've been waiting for?"

"Searching for, more like. But no, not him. The Texan. Wants to meet me in London, tomorrow."

"That sounds like a very bad idea."

"I know. But I figured, one bad idea, why not two?" Vic's phone gave a muffled ping from her purse. "And that must be him. I'll see you on Friday."

"Ah, Ms. Vic. I can't. It will have to be Monday. I need

to go see the imam in Stokes Croft on Friday."

"Oh," replied Vic. "Anything I should know?"

"No, Ms. Vic. I am helping a friend convert to Islam. I am the sponsor. Some formalities that need to be addressed."

The way Rahim covered his mouth with a hand on the word 'friend' made Vic wonder. None of her business. "Maybe you could come in Sunday, then?" She asked. "I'll come too. We'll sort out the backlog. And talk about your dreams of a furniture empire. And maybe other dreams as well." Vic left Rahim holding the glue gun. She ran down the stairs, out the door to the White Hart.

– § –

"Aaugh," grunted George. "This is what fourth phase Internet feels like."

"Is that like the next thing after Web 3.0?" Fatima put a light hand on his back.

"Totally different," replied George, unhunching into her hand from his laptop. "Web 3.0 wasn't even 3.0. It was the same old 2.0, just more of it, with a bit of crypto-NFT pixie dust to fool people into thinking it was genuinely new. Phases. Phase one Internet was green screens and newsgroups. Only a few people had access. It was mainly for research, and some whimsical experiments. Phase two was websites, which were mostly a dog's breakfast. And no way to find anything, unless you typed in exactly the right address. Phase three was when we got organized. Yahoo, Google, Northern Lights, even Bing, God help us. Once it got indexed and widely used, governments, NGOs, and corporations started putting massive amounts of information online. That was genuinely useful. Even without Wikipedia, you could usually find what you wanted."

"So what's phase four?"

"Where we are in right now. A complete mess. Clickbait, phishing, adverse algorithms, AI generated nonsense. The websites of the world have lost the plot. Most are simply schemes to sell you something, chockers with ads. My least favourite is a cunning spelling close to the site you want, complete with content that hides the fact that they're not really what you think they are. Please promise me you'll never visit houseoflords.com. The real House of Lords website is very different. And search is spoiled. Half the links are sponsored or promoted. What you do find is often paywalled, especially if it's any good. And then there are the search databases, where people offer to provide you, for a fee, information that used to be readily available. Don't get me started on the endless videos that promise to reveal the MOST IMPORTANT SECRET, if you keep watching."

"Some of those are actually quite fun, in an intellectually incoherent way." Fatima gave her husband a squeeze on the shoulder.

"I know, love, but mostly it's a massive waste of time. Which is what this was."

"Nothing, eh?"

"Nothing about Sellen & Sellen we didn't already know. Hugh's gone missing, nobody cares. A few mentions of proceedings. Court records are bloody hard to access, unless you're a lawyer or pay a service. But I don't think they'd reveal much, in any event. Josh DeVilliers is exactly what he appears to be. Sharp lawyer on the make, involved in something above his intelligence band. Too bad for us."

"Too bad for him as well," replied Fatima. "Vic will sort him out."

– § –

Vic still didn't like mornings, but the pleasant memory of last night's dinner with Fabio made this one easier. She drove along the M4, nodding in time to one of George's hair metal playlists. "Here I am," she sang along, "Rock you like a hurricane." She touched the kasimala under her grey hoodie. Its weight on her chest was a familiar comfort. Why she had taken it off before dinner with Fabio, she wasn't sure. Heavy gold too much for the dress? She'd put it back on the minute she got home. Alone. She needed it for Dan, she thought. Although how much armour could a necklace be? Her spastic mental chatter organised as she got closer to the boat club, focused on the coming dive, filling the gaps in her now mostly instinctive navigation of London traffic. Better not be any nasties in the brown soup today – she was in no mood for an anemone hijacking.

Vic needn't have worried. Anticipation meant that she huffed her tank faster than usual, but it was a useless, swirling, low visibility day in the river. Nothing much to do but hyperventilate, which gave her a bit more time to get ready for her, what would you call it? Appointment? Interview? Rude summoning, she decided, as she toweled herself dry in the boat club changing room. The drysuit was still quite solid and well-sealed, but worth a shower and a proper change before seeing scary man.

She took the Tube to the Eye. The electric van didn't have to pay the congestion charge, which made London deliveries a lot more friendly, but parking in

Westminster was a congestion charge by itself. A short walk in smart boots from Waterloo station, she was surprised to realize she'd arrived before the 4:45pm reporting time of the QR code. Gave her time to look around for Dan. Score one for the culture, she thought, clocking the smattering of brown faces in the queue. And the long appraising look from the handsome Caribbean who scanned her phone. He had given her a sly smile, accompanied by the slightest of nods, when Private Pod popped up on the scanner. "Your host will be wit you shortly", he'd said, some islands in his accent. A little too young, she thought, but nice to get the action. Was this the Fabio effect?

She watched a group large enough to test the "Max Capacity: 28 persons per Pod" sign of Pod Seven jostle towards the capsule entrance while she waited. She felt a light touch on the shoulder. "Is it time?" she asked.

"Yes, Victoria, it's time," replied a youngish, ruddy-faced man. Clean-shaven, only the eyes gave Dan away, a faint gold ring around the pupils. And the level stare of someone who has looked too long at the world.

"Dan!" she said. "Nice suit." He had dressed up as well, in a banker's uniform of tailored navy, white shirt, conservative tie, the long coat, highwayman locks and grey beard replaced by a fashionably short haircut and reconfigured jawline. It was a slimmer, tighter look, flesh smoother around the eyes, nose a bit more sculpted. Still recognizably Dan, if you had happened to have been a close friend of the younger version of him, which made Victoria wonder if Dan had ever had any close friends. "Looking...." The phrase which popped into her head was "like you're wearing a disguise", but since that would be rude, she simply trailed off.

"Different?" he finished for her. "A little bit. Helps to mirror the money men when you're talking with them about money." Even the accent was muted, long Texas vowels made shorter, elided consonants pronounced more distinctly. "Shall we?" Dan gestured towards the arriving deck of Pod Eight.

Vic noticed with dismay that the pods didn't stop for boarding. The giant wheel continued its slow rotation, the boarding plank of the pod making a slow traverse along the shallow risers of the embarkation ramp, safety doors open. That explained some of the chaos of the group before them, shifting with the steady movement of the capsule. Much easier being only two. Dan strode past the bench in the middle to the far end of the pod. Victoria stepped on board more gingerly. The handsome attender closed the glass doors behind them with a satisfying thunk. They looked out at the river as they rose.

"Right," said Dan, after a moment. "We've got thirty

minutes of privacy. Let's get to it. What'd she say?"

"I'm sorry?" asked Vic.

"Your momma," replied Dan, some of the Texas back in his voice. "I know you talked to her." Dan turned away from the panorama to face her. "Phillip told me." Vic took an involuntary step back. She caught the back of her knee on the wooden bench, causing her to half-fall, half-sit. Dan took another step towards her.

Vic bounced up off the bench. Dan stood close enough their noses were almost touching. With her boots, they were the same height. She looked into his eyes. They held an angry fire she had seen before, matched by a rising heat in her chest. De-escalate, Vicky, she thought. She smoothed his lapels with her hands. "Really nice suit, Danny. Worsted what? Merino?" She created room with gentle pressure and stepped past him to the floor-to-ceiling glass.

"Alpaca."

"Despite the fact that you're bankrupt?" She kept her gaze on the vista. It was gorgeous, Westminster and the Thames in the late afternoon. Would that they could pretend they were only tourists.

Some things were more important than sightseeing. She turned away from the view. "You're broke, aren't you? Mr. LoneStar Tumblecoin. Beggared, broke and desperate. I bet there was never anyone in Bangalore searching the Internet. You can't afford it. It's been only you, the whole time."

Dan closed his eyes and drew a long breath through his nose before replying. "Well now, missy, it's true I'm down to my last few millions," he said. "But I'm not without resources. And this here is a can't miss scheme to get back to a billion. B."

"Can't miss? Is that why you want Phillip back so badly?" Vic crossed her arms and leaned against the guardrail. "Phillip's going to get you back your money? And then what?"

"And then, nothing," said Dan. "Never you mind what happens after that. You just tell your mother to let him come back, and we're quits."

"Quits? We never had a deal to begin with. Phillip is a killer. My mother is mad. This whole business is insane." The pod lifted them above the level of the nearby office buildings. "I did talk with my mother, nutter that she is. I told her I didn't trust this scheme. But it doesn't matter. She's going to do what she wants, and I'm not going to help you."

Dan took the rail next to Vic and looked out. "Observe with me a while." He waited for Victoria to reluctantly turn. "See them folks out there, walking along the promenade? Lining up for the boats? Scurrying between their tiny homes and their crucial government jobs?

They all want something. A new car. A new job. A better house. A fancier title. A bigger office. Whatever it is, to them it's the most meaningful thing in the world." Dan put his arm around Vic's shoulders, with a pressure that was heavier than friendly. "Up here, they look like ants. Blind ants, driven by a scent on a wind beyond their control. Beyond their understanding, even. Driven by instinct, and habit–"

"And money," interrupted Vic, shrugging his arm off her shoulders with some effort. "Filthy, stupid money. That's all this is about."

"And money," conceded Dan. "Because money is power. What do YOU want, little lady?" Dan looked out over the water. "What if I could give you Mal?"

– § –

One of the unfortunate aspects of the change was that Fabio had lost confidence in his ability to understand feminine dynamics. Not that he'd ever been great at it as a woman. That was one of the many data points that led to the change – he didn't feel like a woman. He contemplated the phone resting the charging pad of his tempered glass desk. He decided he was OK not having the instinct to know whether a real man would tough it out on his own. He could phone a friend. Tracy always had good advice about the ladies.

"Fabio!" Tracy sounded jovial. "I thought we were done with appearances this week."

"We are, Trace, we are. This is something else."

"New contracts?" asked Tracy. "Didn't you say to wait until Arch wins the next round?"

"I did. And he will," replied Fabio. "This isn't about work." Fabio took the phone off speaker. "It's personal."

"Personal, eh?" Fabio heard the clank of weights in the background.

"Yeah. You remember that girl I met at the Hart?"

"Girl? Seemed like a fine drink of woman to me, mate."

"Yeah." An idiot grin flickered on Fabio's face. "She is. We went out for dinner last night."

"And?"

"And I'm not sure. She seemed...agitated about something."

"Something, or someone? Hopefully not you, mate." Tracy managed to stifle most of his chuckle.

"Dunno. She had me drop her back at the Hart. Said she'd call this weekend."

"Well, me boy, you'll know in a few days, won't you?"

"Yeah. But she was definitely nervous about something. I should call her."

"Nooooooo, don't do that. Play it cool, let her call. She

has your number, right?"

"She does."

"I'd say in more ways than one, mate. Do some work. Come by the gym. Work the body, clear the mind. But do NOT call her," said Tracy. "I should get back to the plates. See how we feel on Monday, alright?"

"Thanks, Trace." Fabio put his phone back on the charger. He spun in his office chair. There was definitely something off with Victoria.

– § –

"Dan, that's cruel." The heat in her chest hadn't faded, but the mention of Mal added a cold bitter note in her stomach. "He's gone. The chances of finding him are almost zero. You told me yourself."

Dan pushed off from the guardrail and wandered to the other end of the capsule. Her angry heat left with him, leaving only a leaden ache. He muttered something in a low voice, out of range.

"What was that?" she asked.

"I lied," he repeated, louder. "I lied to you, Victoria. Found him the very same day. A can that hot, it shines like a beacon, if you have a mind to look for it. Course, you got to be payin' attention. Would have been easier if it was Mal out there looking for himself. He was always the best sniffer dog of us all. But the rest of us ain't terrible. Else we wouldn't have survived." The twang had fully treacled back into his speech. "Took a lot of juice to actually pluck the damn thing out of this filthy river, but I have him. Or at least, I have the bottle he trapped himself in. Can't say for sure what kind of shape he's in 'til we let him out."

Vic flew toward Dan. He waved a casual hand and knocked Vic back with an invisible fist. The steel round of the guardrail dug into her kidneys, the pressure holding her against it ten times the weight of Dan's earlier arm. He recrossed the cabin to his captive, nonchalant. "Well, that got your attention," he said. "You gonna behave?"

Vic shook her head and the pressure doubled. The weight on her lungs constricted her breathing. Her chest was hot with effort. Except that diving had made her lungs strong - it wasn't her chest that was burning. It was the necklace, in synch with his approach and retreat. As he kept the pressure on, youth and definition slowly melted from Dan's face. Grey threads emerged in his hair. His cheeks pouched. The pressure increased, her lungs on fire within and without. She gave a cautious nod. The pressure vanished, leaving only the radiator warmth of the necklace. Vic sagged against the rail, now a support instead of vise.

"Wise move, Vicky. 'Bout time you showed some sense." A more familiar Dan sat on the wooden bench in the middle of the pod, legs splayed. "You were beginning to wear me out." Dan rubbed at his head and some of the grey disappeared. "Let me tell you how it's going down.

"I'm gonna make you an offer. You're gonna accept. And we are NOT gonna do this again. Got it?" Another slow nod from Vic. "Thought so. Here's the deal. You call your momma back, tell her we spoke. You've changed your mind. Now IS the right time for Phillip to come back, because me, Dan, I've got everything arranged. You and I will be waiting for him, Saturday morning, eleven o'clock. I've got a little house. 12 Harrows Close, Hornchurch. Once Phillip shows up and gives me what I want, I'll give you back your old man in a bottle. Now you nod one more time."

"I would if I could." Vic's voice was a ragged whisper. "Lilith told me she would ignore me if I called again."

"Yeah, well, that woman lies like a tombstone. But gettin' through to her ain't my problem. It's yours. You want to see your man again, get your brother to Harrows Close on Saturday. Everything else is talk." Dan patted his cheeks and stood. His face was almost back to the look she'd encountered when he arrived at the Eye. "Now," he continued, "they say you can get a good view of St. Paul's dome. We're about to be on the way down.

You better find it quick."

– § –

It was hard to concentrate, having to pee all the time. Fatima was trying to file an analysis piece on the anniversary of the return to power of the Taliban, but the baby factory was getting annoying. Her nips hurt. She'd managed the general anxiety and queasiness somewhat OK. Who wasn't miserable and anxious these days? But God, she would kill for an hour of clear thinking. Even forty-five minutes. Between the hormones, the tiredness, and the trips to the WC, she was lucky if she got thirty minutes of decent work done in a regular day. And she wasn't even showing. How could she? According to the ultrasound, the thing was hardly the size of an apple. Which meant that everyone she hadn't told thought she was depressed. They were constantly calling to check in, or texting 'good news' messages. Talk about getting on her tits. As if the Taliban wasn't enough to drive a person mad.

George had the good sense to slope off during the day. He could work from home if he wanted, but he was happier in the van. Or elbow deep in an electrical conduit, she thought, pile of fibre optic at his feet. Certainly better off in a cable tray than hanging around the rim of her emotional volcano. In theory it gave her more time to think, but in practice, his being out and about provided yet another thing for her mind to wander to. As if she needed more. Lately all she could think about was the massive vanity of bringing a child into this current version of the world. Were they doing the right thing? It's not like she would get an abortion now. They had known the odds of what would happen when they stopped using protection. The problem wasn't the baby, it was the job. Fatima was paid to look at the world with a critical eye. There was an awful lot to critique.

This business with Sberbank was another worry, especially with Vic still right in the middle of it. Fatima checked the time on her Disney watch. George had bought it for her so she wouldn't constantly check her phone, being all too easy to look for one thing and get lost in the distracto-ball of notifications and news articles. The watch was stylish enough, small and light, its face dominated by a somewhat angry looking space alien. That was definitely a message, if an affectionate one. Well, he was her space alien too. If having a baby with him was a bit irresponsible, so be it. Just gone half five. Where was this girl?

NO DOWNSIDES

The wheel turns, Fatima vows revenge, Vic reconsiders

Vic shivered in the damp tunnel beneath Westminster Bridge. She'd sat on the pod's wooden bench for the rest of the ride, silent, arms wrapped tightly about herself. Dan maintained a mindless patter, his accent smoothing into a vague trans-Atlantic, before closing with another mild threat and reminder about their deal. The moment the pod door opened, she stepped off the ramp and kept going.

The Queen's Walk was mostly empty in the early evening, tourists having worn themselves out, the first wave of commuters sticking to surface streets and more direct ways home. Vic used the emptiness to be brisk, hard steps punishing the pavement, heedless of Big Ben and Parliament illuminated by a magnificent autumn sun.

Coming out of the tunnel, Vic was confronted by a wall of hearts. Painted red hearts covered the embankment's stone surface. Most had names written inside them, Jamie, Alan, Salman, Ann. Some just said Mum, or Gran. A few were empty. Their imperfect geometry made clear each heart had been hand drawn. Vic stopped to touch the blank space between two hearts. Red hearts, some fading to pink, stretched around the corner and down the Queen's Walk. Thousands of hearts. Hundreds of thousands. A large black plaque announced 'The National Covid Memorial Wall'. She walked more slowly down the wall, reading the names that were there, filling in a few of the empty ones in her mind.

Vic used to fantasize that the virus might turn your skin a bright colour, perhaps violet. Some obvious signal – infected person, stay away. Although violet would only work well for white people. What colour would she and Rahim be? Maroon? They were all red on the inside, a fact the fading hearts made powerfully clear. It had come to each one of them, the main clue just a cough, and coughs have many reasons. Which meant every tickle in the throat added to the constant low-grade fear. Fear, and anger that our collective powerlessness had been made so raw and obvious. The anger that, long past the availability of vaccines, lingered in bad driving and a general degradation of manners. A fear that ebbed and rebounded. Never quite out of mind, but mostly in the back of it, after boosters and new beginnings. Except when you had to walk past heart after aching heart.

The pandemic had touched Vic less than many. She'd lost her father well before it hit. Rahim had an uncle who died of it. He'd been old and overweight, riddled with diabetes. But alive, until a slight cough turned into respiratory distress, and then multiple organ failure. This was the early days, before the vaccine, so they couldn't have a funeral. The family wasn't even allowed to attend the burial. A mortuary assistant in full protective clothing took the body away. They had a virtual prayer service. It was the best they could do. They didn't mourn properly until a year later, when they visited the grave on his death anniversary. Each heart on the wall was someone. Vic continued along the wall. Bryan. Denise. Upendra. Eileen. Why not Mal as well? Vic pounded one of the faded hearts with her fist. How badly did she want him back? Maybe the thing to do was to say goodbye. She walked onward, line of hearts accompanying her.

Fatima's phone finally rang at six o'clock. "Bloody Vixen, I thought you were dead."

"Yeah, that's how I feel, too," replied Victoria. "You

were right."

"Not for the first time," said Fatima. "About what?"

"About Dan being broke. I called him on it, and he admitted it. He wants Phillip back so he can get his money back. Somehow. And he found Mal."

"What?" asked Fatima. "Come again?"

"He found Mal. He has him, Fats." Vic's voice got thick. "In his little bottle."

"Oh, Vixen, aren't we the prize fools. Of course he does. He's magic. That bastard. If he doesn't hand him over, I'm going to kill him. Dan, that is. I'm going to chop off his bollocks and feed them to him. I'm going to–"

"It's not that easy." Vic coughed. "He said he'd give me Mal back if I talk to Lilith, convince her to let Phillip come back."

"Oh." Fatima grew quiet on the line. "That is tricky." Victoria could feel gears turning in Fatima's head. "Listen, where are you, Vix?"

"End of the Lambeth bridge. Thought about throwing myself off, but I swim the Thames too well now to drown."

"Can you leave your van parked overnight at the boat club?" asked Fatima.

"Sure, as long as you don't mind being up early. I have to shift it by six, before the morning rush."

"Ha! I'll be up all night in any event. I'm on deadline

for this Afghanistan article. You can take the Tube. We should talk. George will be home in a tick. We'll send him out for the takeaway this time. Come over. This piece is due tomorrow, and I've got fuck all except for a poetic description of bearded men in shirt dresses doing the Islamic version of the circle dance. See you shortly."

Vic hadn't taken the Tube at peak hour in a very long time. It wasn't Tokyo train stuffer level, but certainly closer to sardines-in-a-tin than she preferred or was used to. The crush of people did keep her from dwelling in her own thoughts, too much work hanging on to the grab-handles, too many looks to avoid, too many stiff and unpleasant bodies she didn't want to touch. For an hour, the only thing that registered was a stark poster stating 'Leprosy is Completely Curable' on the curved wall of the Finsbury Park platform. Which was a good thing, as she might otherwise have forgotten to change trains.

George was pacing the pavement in front of the maisonette. Vic spotted him before he saw her. The vintage British Telecom anorak was a giveaway, rich deep blue with a classic logo. What varied and strange efforts we put into clothes, Vic thought, the uniforms we don to protect ourselves from the world. The cute grey check skirt she thought would give her confidence was a little cold as the day ebbed away. And her feet were starting to kill. These boots were made for walking slightly shorter distances, apparently. "Hey, Georgie," she called out, far enough away not to startle. "Tea for a traveller whose dogs are barking?"

Once inside, George repaired to the kitchen. Vic sat in the one armchair and removed her boots, rubbing her stockinged feet. Tea cup noises and the first cavitation of the kettle bubbled out from where George had disappeared to. Fatima was summoned by the twin alarms of front door rattle and boiling water. She descended the stairs with none of her usual dexterity, one hand on the banister, the other on her lower back. Vic watched her royal progress with amusement. Reaching the base, Fatima unfolded the tray leant against the overcrowded coffee table, then arranged herself cross-legged on the couch, one leg at a time. Comfortably settled, elbows on thighs, Fatima favoured Vic with an enquiring look. All Vic could do was lift her chin. They waited for George in silence. He returned with a familiar tea service and a quizzical expression.

Fatima blinked first. "So, Vixen, how do we get your very old man back?"

"Not sure we do," replied Vic.

"Oh, Victoria, you must!"

"Must I? I'm not convinced." Vic removed the

scrunchy from her hair and shook it out. "Much as it hurts, perhaps I should give up on Mal before more people die. It's a terrible idea to deal with our man Dan. He's not trustworthy. He TOLD me he lies. What if he doesn't even have Mal? He's bad. Very bad. In fact, he's one of them. The necklace told me so. It reacted to him in exactly the way he had warned me about. I think he's desperate."

"Vix. That is a bit scary." Fatima touched her belly as if to check it was still there. "He was dangerous before, and desperate people are even more dangerous. But hear me out. There is no downside. Phillip is dumb enough to come back even if you don't talk to your mum. So do it. Worst case, you don't get Mal, which is how it is now. Best case, your village gets its other idiot back." Fatima reached awkwardly for one of the mugs George had set on the tray. "I thought you were doing all this diving because you wanted him back. Dan and Phillip will likely bugger off and leave us alone. What would they want with us? You told me yourself the most probable thing is that Dan kills Philip."

"Yeah, I'm not excited about that either."

"Oh, Vic," sighed Fatima. "People die every day. I'm going to be up half the night trying to write sensitively about the thousands of people mutilated or slaughtered by the Taliban since they came back, and trying to pick photographs without, you know, violating the dignity of their victims. You want to look at death with me? I know exactly what it is. Anyone who covers Afghanistan, or Syria, or Myanmar, or half a dozen other places, they see pictures of dead children every day. And so many more die unseen. I would put any one of the commanders who ordered the bombing of a school to death tomorrow, and not miss a wink. Phillip killed how many people?"

"More than one, Fats. But I'm not the Taliban."

"Sure, fine, but you have been living under a fatwa for the last three years. There's a reason there's a gun under your bed. About time you did something useful with it."

George sprayed a mist of tea over the papers littering the coffee table. "I'm sorry," he spluttered. "Who is this person I married? Bloody Mary?"

"Not quite, my love," replied Fatima, wiping her cheek. "But not Lady Di either. I'm serious. Vic should do this, even if it means her brother shuffles off his not particularly mortal coil."

"What if I can't?" asked Vic. "I mean, what if I can't get through to Lilith?"

"How do you mean?" asked both George and Fatima.

"I mean, Mum essentially told me to get stuffed. She said she was going to ignore me until she found out more on her own."

"Hmm." Fatima adjusted herself on the couch. "Bold

talk. She's your mother. I'm sure she's listening somehow."

"Perhaps," said Vic. "She said I could 'assemble my friends at the points of the star'."

"Right." Fatima almost bounced in her seat. "Then that's what we'll do. We'll need five people. You, me, Georgie. That's three."

"Rahim," added Victoria. "And I guess I could ask Fabio."

"Your new friend?" 'Friend' from Fatima sounded lascivious.

"Yeah. Who else can I call on short notice?" asked Vic. "Dan wants the reunion on Saturday, which only gives us tonight and tomorrow. I expect Rahim has gone home by now."

"His phone should still be working," said Fatima. "But Friday is better. We use tonight to line up reinforcements. Like that Sellen lawyer. Perhaps we get him to the meet as well. Lawyers make good witnesses."

"Or additional victims," said Vic.

George put down his teacup. "Victoria. Fatima. Josh DeVilliers is in this up to his neck. He may even BE the missing piece of it. I'm with Killer Whale here. Invite him along."

Fatima threw a cushion at him. It bounced off his shoulder, sending one of Fatima's paper towers sliding to the floor. One page stuck on the table, a printout of an old magazine cover. It was a photograph of an Afghan girl whose nose had been cut off by the Taliban.

"Ugh, Fats, why do you have that on the table?"

"Oh, ace, I was looking for that. It's real, unlike Dan's promises, or happy endings. I keep it for inspiration. Which is why we're going to swing into action. Email that lawyer. Call Rahim. George and I will be at your studio tomorrow night. Inspiration, Vic. And revenge!"

Dinner was dismal. They picked at the takeaway with wooden chopsticks and crestfallen expressions. Fatima had had the good sense to stop pushing after Victoria agreed to rally the troops. After a glum hour, George invented an errand to give them a bit of space. Vic decided she'd be better off driving home in the dark than moping around until morning.

Returning to the boat club in the late evening by Tube was more civilized than her previous trip. But her thoughts were louder. The worst was that Fatima was probably right - even if Dan was lying, they should try.

Dan's offer, dangling like a hypnotist's watch, was teasing out feelings she had been avoiding. She didn't like it. Diving had been her refuge. What she really needed was a good shoot, to feel the jerk of the shotgun against her shoulder, smell the burnt powder. Most of all, to watch a paper target shred with angry force. She was angry. Angry at Dan for giving her hope after she'd banked down that lantern to a faint glow. Angry at herself for giving up on Mal after searching for so long. Angrier at herself, because if she was honest, she knew that she had almost reached the point of letting him go on her own. Before Dan returned and upended her life. Again.

She used to dive on every delivery to London. She made Rahim offer free shipping on the website to give her more frequent reason to go. Lately, they were consolidating deliveries, holding onto orders. Turning two or three trips into one. Rahim argued it gave them a better profit margin. Of course it did, as if her trips to the Thames were about margins. It was getting harder to hold a map of the shifting currents in her mind's eye, longer to reacquaint herself with the changing riverbed each dive. Yet she did want him back. He had blown up and reassembled her world, leaving a Mal-sized cubby hole behind the wardrobe door.

Even their fights had been good fights. She'd never been willing to speak her whole mind, to be open about the hurts at the heart of things. She'd fought with past boyfriends about their habits, about money, about the unbelievable drivel that came out of their mouths, but always with only one barrel of the gun. Mal she gave everything. Other lovers had ignored the overfull dustbin, which annoyed her no end, yet she had rarely said anything. The first time Mal balanced something on top of an already full bin, she told him that she didn't want to feel like she was alone in the world.

As he'd emptied it, he'd said, "I note that you also have arms and legs. Nice ones, perfectly capable of emptying the bins as well. We both put the rubbish in. I won't be the only one to take the rubbish out." When her eyes had flashed, he'd doubled down. "Your father might have taken care of the rubbish for you. He's dead, and I'm not him. But if this is how I show I love you, well then, amen." He'd raised the bin liner and broke out his cheekiest grin before becoming serious. "Not the most conventional of romantic gestures, but a lot easier to arrange than a midnight stroll through Paris. Could be the start of a trend. Radio call in programmes will ask what one can do to get in the mood. The rustle of bin liner. Then, fwaaaah." He had changed her and changed for her. That was worth at least one more battle.

Late Thursday evening, almost Friday morning, the roads from the bathing club to the motorway were deserted. Vic had never really thought of herself as a physical person, an athlete, someone who lived in the body, of the body. She was an artist. She sketched, she painted, she dreamed up designs. She thought of herself as a creature of the mind. Yet the mechanical work of steering the quiet van through quieter streets gave her solace. She let herself dwell for a few hours in the calming display of competence, manoeuvring the van home, hands steady on the wheel, easy arms made muscular carrying tanks of oxygen to the put-ins on the riverbank and operating the growing set of power tools she and Rahim were accumulating. Rahim. He'd said he'd be off tomorrow. She'd have to disturb him.

SOME ASSEMBLY REQUIRED

Vic nails a first impression, friends come full circle

Vic woke up Friday morning unusually refreshed. She hadn't slept this well in a decade, although it wasn't obvious why. While the general pandemic anxiety had dissipated, she still had a business to run, a murderous conspiracy to foil. It wasn't that the weather had lifted, the constant weather of being Black in England, the looks at and looks past, the assumptions and mis-estimations, the where are you really froms and the why don't you go back theres, the responsibility of representing. As if she had wanted to be spokesperson for and authority on the high-melanin experience. It did have the occasional advantage, like never having to search for the shop assistant since they were always. So. Close. By. And she rather liked her young, gifted, and Black profile in Bristol Magazine. But only when she was able to turn off the part of her brain that whispered being a successful female entrepreneur was not what caught their attention, the part that mourns the exceptionality of being successful while Black in a world that refuses to examine why Black people have to be twice as good to be equal, to fit in and act the 'right way' to be deserving of decency and respect. In a way, it was a relief when Marcus Rashford missed that penalty kick. It made the racism overt. Yet for all that, she felt good. The only explanation she could think of was that the stone of Mal never coming back had finally started to shift. Seemed a pity that the only way to live happily was to think about death.

Her diving instructor had told her to never forget diving was dangerous. The instructor had said that to feel comfortable in the water, Vic must embrace the idea that the thing she was about to do could quite likely kill her. It had sounded very Zen, very Bushido. It wasn't until her first near-fatal accident that she got it. An early summer dive, she'd spotted something bronze and shiny on the river bottom. Fixated, she hadn't notice the current taking her lower. Her fins brushed the bottom, kicking up a cloud of silt. Visibility is never great in the Thames. With this extra contribution, it dropped to zero.

What she should have done was adjust her buoyancy and come up. Or simply dropped her weight belt – weights were cheap. With her weight belt on the bottom, she'd float up to the top. Instead, she tried to turn, dragging her fins through the mud even more. More silt led her to the thing that kills the most divers. Panic. Thrashing her arms to disburse the cloud, she knocked off her mask. Blind, disoriented, lost in fifteen feet of water, she closed her eyes against the gritty muck and sucked hard on the regulator's silicone mouthpiece. Floating at some random angle to horizontal, she had a vision of her dead body drifting past Mal's elusive bronze prison at last. Visualising the places her corpse might go, her heart rate slowed. After a few minutes of not dying, stale air drawing reliably through the mouthpiece, her breath evened. She did an inventory. Mask, gone. Regulator, probably clenched more tightly in her jaw than warranted. Buoyancy compensator, right as rain. She found the auto-inflate button by touch. Extra air lifted her to vertical, the top of her head breaking the surface first. She opened her eyes to find herself in the middle of the channel, fair prey for passing boats. Buoyancy compensator inflated like a life jacket, she lashed at the water with clumsy strokes, splashing to be seen, but also because there was no not-awkward way to swim to the bank, her arms shook through with adrenaline.

That night she slept like a baby. Some of it was plain physical fatigue, the panic and subsequent rush of chemicals through her body having expended a day's worth of energy in minutes. But there was something else beyond that she had nearly died. She had found out what happens when she lost control in the water. And she had learned how to find control again. Her next dive, she was extra careful with her pre-dive checks, proud owner of a new mask and a new unhurried patience. Once in the water, she was serene. It wasn't that there was nothing else that would kill her. There were plenty of ways to get hurt in the Thames, from underwater snags to random oar blades. If anything, it was stupidly dangerous to dive in such a well-trafficked waterway. She still had the fear. But she was no longer afraid.

In a similar way, the idea of Mal being gone forever had unblocked a door in her mind, a door she had painted over and covered with wallpaper. She was keeping it closed for now. But it was no longer hidden. There were the hinges, right there, bulging through the paper covering. The possibility that it could be opened, that there would soon be a time when she was ready to open it, this was enough to give her...something? It wasn't hope. It was as if she could now see the invisible stone she had been carrying around. She didn't need to put it down. She'd carry it a little while longer. Knowing what it was that made her back bow and her feet ache, that was enough.

She thought back to the afternoon in the workshop Rahim had been going on about that Bruce Springsteen movie. He had gone to see it with a friend the previous night. They had only picked it because the main character was a British Muslim. They went in with no clue about the music and fell in love with both the movie and Springsteen. Which had gotten Vic into a stupid fight with Mal later. There was a song in the movie that Rahim had found especially profound. He had quoted it as "is a dream a lie when it doesn't come true?", which didn't sound exactly right to Vic. She had asked Mal about it after she got home. He knew the song, but rather than talk about it, he had gone on a rant about how Vic should always be prepared to move on. He'd said, "You shouldn't think of a dream that doesn't come true as a lie. It's more like a door that closed. You can spend the rest of your life pounding on it, miserable. Or you can open another door. Even dreams that come true eventually run out. Whatever we've had, whatever we have together, time will run out on you and me."

"What do you mean by that?" she asked.

"Well," he said, "I mean we will always love each other. And there may come a time when you need to go love someone else." This was too close to the topic of people Victoria loved dropping dead than she cared to think about. But the metaphor stuck with her.

Vic scrubbed off the melodrama in the shower, threw on clothes, and headed to the studio. George and Fatima would reach around seven. Rahim would join them after he finished his business at the mosque. She had some work to do first.

– § –

It still took courage for Fabio to push on the men's changing room door. As if he hadn't seen a penis before. Or taken off his shirt in public. Still, it was easier to power through a set of deadlifts with a monster bar than fight years of habit and conditioning. Fabio did have to admit, having made the switch, it was amusing to observe the differing styles of his new locker mates. Some guys avoided eye contact and wrapped their kit in a towel before dropping trou, which felt familiar. Others struck up conversations whose main point seemed to be how comfortable they were naked. Fabio's primary technique was boxer shorts on gym days, change in the toilet cubicle or shower at home. Half-naked was fine. He'd always had small nipples for a girl. Shirtless, his pecs and delts were as ripped as anyone. He might take a little bit of ribbing about grandad pants, but strength spoke to strength.

Fabio didn't spend a lot of time in the changing room. He was there to get the work in, to enjoy the instinctive kinship of serious gym rats. It was how he met Tracy, and why Archie trusted him. And why he trusted Tracy, for that matter, although trust and bravery aren't the same. He and Tracy worked wordlessly through three rotations of squats, lifts, and lunges before Fabio decided to speak up.

"Trace. I got a text."

"First one ever, eh?"

"Rare form, Trace," replied Fabio. "From the girl, the one who said she'd call me this weekend."

Tracy gave a positive grunt. "Good stuff. Told you to play it cool. What'd she say?"

"She wants me to meet some of her friends."

"Even better." Tracy racked his last set of plates. "You telling me to brag, or what?"

"She wants me to meet some of her friends, TONIGHT."

"Friday night, sounds alright," said Tracy.

"It would be, if I didn't have the women's boxing match in Swansea this evening. She said weekend. I thought that meant Saturday and Sunday."

"Some folks start the weekend on Thursday night, mate. Skip the boxing, go have a good time." Tracy headed to the treadmills to start his cool-down.

Fabio hopped on a vacant treadmill next to Tracy. "I can't. It's a Board of Control event. I'm repping a real contender in the undercard," said Fabio. "If she wins, she can challenge for a title."

"Is she fit?"

"You saw her. She's gorgeous."

"I meant the boxer. Does she have a chance?"

"Oh, yeah, maybe. It's a bit of a tossup. Her opponent is getting on a bit, but still an Olympic medalist. At forty. Not bad."

Tracy increased the incline of his treadmill. "What about you?" asked Tracy.

"What about me what?" Fabio looked up from the controls.

"Do you have a chance?"

"Dunno. Maybe about the same as my boxer. Said she needed me come to her studio tonight and meet her friends."

"She said 'need'?"

"My phone is in the locker, but, yeah, I think she said 'need you to come'."

"Oh, mate, you're in. I can look after the boxer for you."

"I shouldn't. It's not professional."

"Professional." Tracy looked at his friend. "What's more important, love or money?"

"Trace, don't ask me questions I shouldn't answer. I am a sports agent, you know."

"Yeah, I know. An agent who's going to pay me to

drive to Swansea and watch the boxing. Text me the details."

"Oh, mate, this one better be worth it."

"Sounds like she already is."

– § –

Rahim was right about the studio. They were really backed up, too few workers to match demand. A barbarian army of part-built pieces occupied most of the room. Victoria did a quick triage of what she might possibly finish before the gang showed up. Not much. Too many orders half started, then neglected while she went out on dates and back and forth to the Big Smoke. Well, she thought, the only way to finish is to start. She picked one of the simpler cabinets and lost herself in assembly. She was startled by an angry hunger pang somewhere in the late afternoon. Had she really been grafting for six hours? She had three finished sticks as evidence. One of the things she hated most was crating pieces before they had a chance to completely dry, but, got to make room. Perhaps the varnish won't be tacky after a quick sandwich break. At minimum, it would give a chance for the fumes to clear. Or at least, clear her head.

She found Fabio looking lost in the lobby on her return. The reception desk unstaffed promptly at six. Vic always struggled to remember the name of the temps. Mary? Marnie? Anyway, the temp wasn't here and Fabio was. Vic gave a shy wave and a dab at her face to check for stray sauce. "Hiya." Bold greeting, she thought. Totally the right foot.

"Hi, Victoria." Fabio's voice was warm and light. He wore a plain t-shirt under a slim fit suit in contrasting shades of blue.

"Is that linen?" asked Vic, fingering the lapel. At least they were both wearing t-shirts, although in hindsight, the faded Free Tibet t-shirt Victoria had stolen from Fatima was probably a size too small for the occasion. Sod it, she thought. No need to explain the rips and stains on her jeans, either. This was how she dressed for work. "You're early," she said, before Fabio could reply. "And well turned out."

"Yeah, semi-formal." Fabio gave an apologetic shrug. "I was supposed to be going to an event tonight."

"Oh, changed your plans for me?" asked Vic.

"Not really." Fabio straightened up. "Thought I had a ticket, but my friend decided to go instead. It's not a bother I'm early? After I finished at the gym, thought I'd come straight over rather than fiddle about or go home. Maybe see what you do?"

"Yeah, it's fine." Vic went up the stairs, not waiting to see if Fabio followed. "I could use some help before the others get here." Vic unlocked the door and was inside before Fabio reached the upstairs corridor. "In here," she called out.

Fabio stopped at the studio entrance, Vic's back to him. She was surrounded by chaos, hands on hips. The floor was criss-crossed with sawdust tracks. Four bulky shapes concealed by white drop cloths stood sentry in a ragged line across the back half of the room. Behind Vic's trim silhouette, in the centre of the room, was a half-assembled packing crate. Its parts lay prostrate around the base of a majestic oak display case, sides fanned out, worshipers at the cabinet altar. "This is NOT how I intended to introduce you to my work." Vic turned to face him, scratching her hairline. "Or my friends. But I'm glad you've come. You're needed."

Fabio didn't know what to make of that last statement. Perhaps keep it simple. "My pleasure, Victoria."

"Good stuff," she replied. Pointing to a spare hook among racks of tools, she said, "You can put your nice jacket there and help me crate this up."

"Sure. But can I get a look first?" Fabio gingerly stepped his elegant loafers around the major dust lines on the floor, leaving faint marks in the finer layer coating the floor like flour in a bakery. He made a clover of footprints around the sides of the packing crate. "This is for....?"

"Guns, mostly," replied Vic.

"Didn't realize you were so martial," he said.

"Yeah, picked it up during the pandemic. Felt good to be outside blasting away at something. And for self-defense."

"Something I should know?" asked Fabio.

"That I can take care of myself?" Vic knelt and busied herself with a small black duffel. "Some people buy this model for fishing rods. Or swords. But it's mainly rifles and shotguns." She lifted a complicated looking assembly out of the duffel bag. "And occasionally nail guns. Can you grab that pallet?" Vic nodded her head at a wooden flat leant against the wall.

"Is this a yoga mat?" Fabio sank his thumb into the layer of rubber foam fixed to the pallet top.

"Yeah, I get the worn-out ones free from a local studio. Then cut and glue. Cheaper and better than new material." With Fabio's help, Vic positioned the pallet mat-side-down on top of the gun cabinet and aligned its sides to a twin already underneath. "Hold it steady." She put the nail gun on the pallet top and crouched, using both hands to lever the first flat side of the crate up from the floor. She pressed it fast against the bottom pallet with one foot and held the top with her shoulder. The "pop-pop-pop" of the nail gun sounded like real gunshots in the enclosed space, startling Fabio. Fortunately, the three nails held it secure. She bent at the waist and put a matching three in the bottom. "Sorry, should have warned you," she said, straightening up. A smile turned her face into a sun-dappled river. "But I did say 'steady' for a reason." She pointed her chin at the next one on the floor. "Can you lift that for me?"

Fabio reached down with one hand and lifted the second crate side, sinews flashing ridges and valleys in his arm. Bulges appeared and disappeared in his shoulder as the crate side reached vertical. Vic moved around him to nail the second side into place. She gave a friendly pat to his lower back as they readied the third side. "I guess that gym work can be handy."

"Aren't you going to ask me if I like the piece?" asked Fabio.

"Not really. It's a professional gun cabinet. Not a ton of design in it. Good finish, if the varnish doesn't catch on the yoga mat. We do one of these every other week." Vic motioned with her eyes. Fabio lifted and Vic nailed the last side of the packing crate. "All we're doing right now is making room. Back in a tick." She left Fabio holding the crate.

A low rumble from the hall outside brought Vic popping back, yellow pallet jack in tow behind her. She slotted the forks of the jack into the hollows of the pallet base with the ease of many repetitions. "Mind the store while I take this to the van?" asked Victoria. She vanished again, the grinding of the jack wheels reverberating into the studio from the hall.

"Um, sure," replied Fabio, his voice echoing in the slightly emptier room. A four-armed starfish silhouette of unassembled crate remained in the dust of the middle of the room, one arm scarred by the tracks of the departed pallet. The ding of a lift door marked Victoria's progress outside. Low, drop cloth covered objects of mystery beckoned.

The first was an early version of the piece they had packed up, unstained wood and only part-assembled. A glassless door leaned against the front, to be secured with hinges at some later date. Fabio re-covered it with the drop cloth and moved to the next shape, lower and wider. Some kind of bar or liquor cabinet, almost done, deep grooves awaiting inlays. A filigree mesh front swung open at Fabio's touch, invisibly hinged at the side with cunning craft. The top hinges were more obvious. When opened, the top revealed mysterious half-circles marked in faint pencil across the back and shelves. Drains? Outlets? Fabio could tell only that it was a handsome piece, with solid parts and cleanly fitted joints. Instead of four feet, it stood on six, an extra pair of gilded feet in front the decorative base for two bold columns carved directly into the wood of the door. Fabio gently lowered the lid and closed the front. This had taken hours of work. Wouldn't make good odds for a next date if he destroyed it.

Vic was back and next to him before Fabio could uncover the third. She seemed to have a ninja knack for sneaking into her own studio. "Hey," she said. "What are you doing?"

"Looking at your nice bits," replied Fabio. "What did you expect?"

"Better security. But I got to watch you for a minute." Vic's expression was softer than her tone. "You like them."

Fabio tilted his head to one side. "Well," he said, "I might if they were finished. We'll see by how much they improve when you're done."

"Rascal." Vic laughed. "Help me shift them. And we'll need to sweep up as well. It's a complete tip in here."

Fatima and George walked in on a giant pentacle dominating the studio floor. Dusk had robbed the light from the clerestory windows. Tools and bags were tidied away, parts hung on racks, part-works shifted into a neat heap in one corner, chairs pushed under the desk. Fabio and Victoria had traced a chalk circle six metres in diameter, then inscribed it with a five-pointed star, a pentagram. Fabio sat barefoot in the middle, t-shirt dusty with chalk and damp with sweat. He raised a chalk-stained hand. "Hi. You must be Fatima and George."

"He's George. I'm Fatima. Who are you?"

Fabio gave as much of a bow as he could manage cross-legged. "Fabio. Sports agent to the stars. Friend of Victoria."

"Where is she?" asked Fatima.

"On a pizza run. She figured you'd be hungry."

"She's right about that," said Fatima. "All I do now is eat and sleep."

"And write. Is that Afghan story out?" Vic appeared at the door, a stack of white boxes in her arms.

"Hey, Vicky." Fatima touched her elbow to Vic's arm. "Nope. Submitted, but the paper's sitting on it until the weekend edition." Fatima hooked a thumb at Fabio in the circle. "Who's this joker?"

"Fabio. I told you about him."

"Oh, I know who he is," laughed Fatima. "I wanted to see what you'd say in front of him."

"Cheeky." Victoria put the boxes down on her desk. George unstacked them and peeked curiously inside.

Fabio rose and stepped cautiously over the chalk lines to assist. "Fabio, meet my obnoxious friend Fatima–"

"Call me Fats."

"And her husband, George," continued Vic.

"Hiya," said George, his nose in a box.

"If you're obnoxious and Fatima," asked Fabio, his face carefully neutral, "does that make you...Foxy?"

"It makes me pregnant, moody, and starving," replied Fatima. "What goodies has Vixen got for us, George? Although I do like Foxy and Vixen. Perhaps you can keep this one, Vicky." Fatima powered on. "Does he know what you've gotten him into? I mean, George and I have taken one of these nap times before. Hopefully you explained who you were drawing the circle for. Although I have to say, the star is a nice touch. Neat work."

"Yeah, haven't gotten that far," said Vic.

"Two margherita, an anchovy and olive, and...is that potato on the fourth one?" asked George.

"Any plates? Or are we still poor starving students who eat out of the box?" Fatima tore free a small slice. "Still warm. And tasty," she said, between bites.

"There's some kitchen roll in the drawer," said Vic.

"Um," Fabio cleared his throat. "Something I should know?"

Victoria faced him, registering with delight that with Fabio barefoot, she was a smidge taller. "Oh, usual stuff.

Fatima is my best friend since a very long time. George I had my doubts about but it was simply my foolishness. He's hopelessly devoted to Fatima and handy besides."

"Hey!" said George and Fatima, almost in synch.

Fabio put his hand on Vic's waist. "No, I meant, the significance of the circle you've had me help you draw. Your best friend here seemed to imply I was in for something…" Fabio couldn't find the right word. Menacing? Unusual? Unpleasant? There was a distinct downside implied, despite Fatima's offhand tone.

"Right." Vic put her hand on Fabio's and let it rest there. "How to explain. We're, uh, going to have a collective out-of-body experience. You see, normal daughters, if someone was as interested as you obviously are, they might talk to their Mum about it. But she's no longer of this Earth, so we try something different."

"Vic, that's not exactly a full description of what's about to happen," said Fatima.

"Fats, I'm not entirely sure what's about to happen," said Victoria. "There's a good chance we'll all feel a big nothing."

"Drugs?" asked Fabio.

"No drugs," replied Vic. "Look, here's the plan. I know it's going to sound a little strange. My father is dead. My mother is…not here anymore. But I sometimes have these hyper-vivid dreams where I can talk to her. It only seems to work if I'm really agitated, and I have a group of people with me. When Rahim gets here, we're going to lie down as five on the points of the star, hold hands, and try to fall asleep. If it works, we'll have some crazy shared dream–"

"The last one was on a boat. Or rather, a shipwreck," added Fatima.

Vic gave her friend the side-eye. "We'll lie down, have some crazy dream, and then we'll wake up. Should be harmless fun. Don't let the pizza get cold."

Fatima stamped her foot. "Vixen, you should warn him about Dan."

"Right," said Fabio. "Who's Dan?"

NOT MUCH OF A HONEYMOON

Josh cuts the line, Rahim crosses it, Vic rides a dark horse, or something like it

Josh was not in the habit of answering unknown numbers. Nor of answering the phone at mealtimes. They had waited a month for this reservation, and he wasn't about to ruin it by taking out his phone. Why his wife had demanded "degustation", he wasn't entirely sure. If only the caller would go away – these little plates were delicious. He furtively looked at his phone under the table. Four missed calls from the same number. His wife tapped his foot gently with a Gucci pump. An anonymous server had changed his empty plate for a small porcelain bowl.

"Josh, it's the palate cleanser," his wife said. "Taste the sorbet and then take your call outside. It must be important." His wife made a go-on motion with her head. "But be quick, please."

Josh hit the call button before he reached the door of the dining room. The other party answered immediately.

"One sec," said Josh, manoeuvring around a foursome in dinner jackets and gowns. The autumn air was bracing compared to the warmth of the dining room. "Hello?"

"Jawshhhhh." A long drawl from the other end. "It's Dan. Firestone. From your office, the other day."

"Yes, I'm aware of who you are," replied Josh.

"Good, son, good. I've got the password. But if you want to get paid, I need you to come to London tomorrow."

Josh heard plates being exchanged behind him. "Yes, yes, 12 Harrows Close, I'm planning on it."

"Say what, son?"

"Is that not correct?" asked Josh.

"Naw, you got the address alright. Just, I hadn't told you it yet."

"I got the message from Victoria. Now, look, they're serving the next course. I really do have to go. We can talk more tomorrow."

"I'm the one who's supposed to hang up on you," said Dan. But no one was listening.

– § –

Rahim's companion was so pale, it was shocking she didn't have red hair. It was hard to tell what shade of brown she did have under the gauzy pink hijab. Pretty in an unremarkable way, with an upturned nose. Orange freckles and Taylor Swift red lipstick added character to otherwise washed-out features. The headscarf and lipstick contrasted against the grey long-sleeved maxi that covered her wrist to ankle. Vic's first thought was that Rahim had tried, and succeeded, at finding the polar opposite of his boss and business partner.

"This is Maryam," said Rahim, holding her hand but looking down at the floor. The pair stood in the hall in front of the open studio door, seeming to have no intention of coming in.

Vic waved them to enter. "When I said 'the door is open', Rahim, I meant, cross the threshold." Vic sketched a quick greeting. "Salaam, Maryam. Join us, please. Nice to meet you." Vic took a quick glance around the room. "This is Fatima. Her partner George. Over there is Fabio. And on that desk should be a few spare slices of pizza. Cold, I'm afraid. I'm Victoria."

"Yes, I know," said Maryam. "I work the reception downstairs. Cold is fine – I'm starving. Rahim was so insistent we come quickly he wouldn't let me grab a single bite after mosque." Maryam stepped around the chalk circle and rifled through the pizza boxes.

Rahim shyly closed the door. Everyone else watched Maryam. A crystal hair pin winked as she hitched the trailing end of her hijab away from the grease. Vic crossed the chalk line to help Maryam find a last piece. "Um, sorry, I didn't recognize you."

"It's alright," said Maryam. "Nobody remembers the temps. Except Rahim."

"Speaking of Rahim," said Vic, cornering him at the door. "You could have told me you couldn't make it."

"I tried," said Rahim, a helpless look on his face. "I told you I was busy. You wouldn't listen."

"Look, Ree, I WAS a bit insistent. But YOU were vague. 'I'm not sure I can come.' What was that? You might have mentioned you were meeting a friend."

Rahim mumbled something inaudible. Maryam, mouth full of pizza, touched Vic's arm. She chewed hard and, mouth still somewhat full, said, "Not friends. Married." Maryam swallowed and added, "Today."

"Oh, shit, Ree." Vic felt blood rush to her cheeks. Must be glowing like a midnight blackberry, she thought. "If I knew you were getting married, I never would have bugged you to come."

"It's ok. We talked about it. The nikah was only with the imam. We'll have a proper reception later." Rahim walked over to his wife. "Maryam thought it was more important to help people who needed me than to make a big fuss."

"Yeah, the big fuss is coming later," added Maryam.

"When we meet the parents."

"Oh, shit. Shit, Ree." Vic gaped at her assistant.

"Yes, Ms. Vic. A whole mountain of it," said Rahim.

"Right, well, good stuff." Fabio found his voice. "Congratulations, Rahim and Maryam. Vic, can we make a toast?"

"Yeah, there's a mini-fridge behind that chair. Not sure if I have cups, though." Vic felt her eyes grow moist. "Everyone, give us a hug. Group cuddle for the happy couple." Vic slung one arm around Fabio and the other around Maryam, who was already holding on to Rahim. Fabio made room for George and Fatima. Vic said, "Rahim, Maryam, I'm so happy for you. Ree, you sly dog." Everyone squeezed in close. "If you don't have a family while your parents work through this, you have a family. Right. Here." Vic gave one more squeeze, eyes a bit moist. As the group disentangled, she saw Rahim and Maryam's eyes were too. Could have been she hugged too tight.

Fabio repositioned two chairs and guided Rahim and Maryam to them. Fatima gave the inside of the unblocked mini-fridge a hard once-over. "Sparkling wine or sparkling apple? I know which one I'M having," she said.

"Champagne, methode, cava, prosecco, whatever it is, I'll take it." said Fabio. "It's a celebration."

"Yeah, wine for me too," said George. "But then we should get to work. It's well past eight."

Celebrating Rahim and Maryam's marriage had scuffed the chalk circle. Fabio and Vic redrew it while George and Fatima lined up the empties by the stack of pizza boxes. Maryam watched from a chair in the far corner as Fatima, George, Rahim, Fabio, and Victoria arranged themselves around the circle. Victoria instructed them to lay flat, heads at the five points of the star, feet towards the centre, hold hands, and close their eyes.

"Then what's going to happen?" asked Fabio.

"Not sure," said Fatima. "It's different every time. Besides, I thought you WANTED to lie down with my friend."

"Shh," said Vic. "Close your eyes and relax. The idea is to fall asleep."

Fabio kept the clever reply he was unable to conjure to himself. He almost always found the perfect thing to say, after the moment had passed. He decided instead to focus on the experience. Vic's hand was warm and a little sweaty. She held his the way a mother might hold the hand of a child. Firm, but with her thoughts on something else. Probably where they were going. Who they were about to meet. Rahim's hand was cool, his grip tentative. The touch of a stranger.

Even a few years in, so much of navigating life for Fabio was gap-filling, faking bonds built between men over a lifetime of shared moments. Some of this was natural. Young men don't need to be taught what it feels like to hold their penis in front of the urinal. The satisfied mastery. My life may be shit, I might be totally hammered, or broke, or both, but I can look down and confirm that I'm the man. A few shakes to remind the world that it's mine.

Fabio squeezed his eyes shut harder and tried to think about something else. He remembered Asian men he'd seen holding hands walking down the street, or arms around shoulders. There was something charming about that innocent, comfortable kinship. Some portion might have been sexual, but mostly it was friendship, the casual bond that comes from a common culture. Vic's touch was like that. Not as intimate as he might like. Fabio squeezed Rahim's hand by reflex. Rahim squeezed back. This is what fear and companionship feel like, he thought. Not quite rugby. But I'll take it.

Four minutes passed. Five. Fabio could feel the circle flexing through the connection of hands, Vic adjusting her grip, Rahim's warming. The back of his head grew cool against the hard floor. Fatima broke the silence.

"Last time," she said, "something happened much faster."

"Yeah," agreed Vic. "Nothing. Not even tired."

"So, Vicky, we keep trying?" asked Fatima.

"Not sure what else we can do," replied Vic. "Mum said to assemble everyone at the points of a star. Maybe we need to think about her harder."

"Think about who?" said Fabio.

"Vic's mum," said Fatima. "Which would be hard, since you've never met her." Fatima let go of George and Victoria to sit up inside the circle. "She's a bit like Vic-"

"I BEG YOUR PARDON," shouted Vic.

Fatima ignored her. "She's kind of like Vic, dark skinned, medium-ish height, good looking, a wee bit angry by default. But older. Think of her as Vic Senior. Right, Georgie?"

George looked around. No cover. "Er, I didn't interact with her much. But there is a family resemblance."

Fatima flashed Vic a triumphant look. "And her name is Lilith. Maybe we call her? You know, chant her name or something."

"Now I think you're taking the piss," said Vic.

"Oh, Vixen, almost constantly, and I would if we had a bit more time. We need Phillip tomorrow. Why not try?"

Fatima lay back down. They joined hands again.

Feeling deeply self-conscious, Vic started calling her mother's name, softly at first. "Lilith. Lilith. Lilith." The others joined in. "Lilith. Lilith. Lilith." The chant grew louder. Maryam shifted in her chair. It was now loud enough that the high ceiling of the studio produced an echo. "Lilith. Lilith. Lilith."

George hadn't ever thought about how hard it was to say "Lilith" over and over. By the twentieth repetition, it was turning into a bit of a tongue-twister. This wasn't how married life was supposed to work out, he thought, lying on your back in a cold room chanting the name of your friend's mother. It was supposed to be cozy couches and cups of tea, pushing a pram, going to work. Couldn't this magic business get over already? "Lilith. Lilith. Thilith."

"Sod it," said Vic. "It's not working." She pushed Fabio and Fatima's hands away and rolled onto her hands and knees. "We go tomorrow without him."

Maryam cleared her throat. "Excuse me."

"Yes, Maryam?" Vic looked up.

"Not all stars have five points," said Maryam. "Some have six."

"What do you mean?"

"I mean, perhaps it's not working because you're only five people. We could try with me."

"Maryam!" said Rahim. "You shouldn't."

"Why not? It's OK enough for you."

"I've been through it before," replied Rahim.

"How many times?"

"One." Rahim looked away.

"And did you know what you were getting into then?" she asked.

"Your point is true," he mumbled. "But how do we add you?"

Vic was already standing. "Everybody up!" she said. "First, we erase the pentacle and draw a star of David."

"The seal of Solomon," added Rahim.

Fabio took off his dusty t-shirt and used it to wipe away the lines of the five-pointed star. "God, your friend is built," stage whispered Fatima.

"Yeah," replied Vic. "He does this on purpose. I'm sure I could have found a cloth somewhere."

"Sure," replied Fatima, "but he's not the only one whose shirt is too small for them. Wasn't that mine?"

Fabio shook out his t-shirt and put it back on, unable to hide a somewhat satisfied grin. Vic hunted for the string she and Fabio used to draw the circle. "George, lend me a hand," said Vic. She found the centre point and George lightly retraced a portion of the arc. He and Vic then swapped roles. George held his end steady while Vic walked a double of the same arc inside the main circle, using George on the edge as her new centre. She motioned for Fatima and Maryam to stand at the points where the new half circle touched the original. She waved Fabio over to the opposite side of the original circle from George. Rahim grasped it immediately, marking the three corners of the first triangle. They quickly drew two equal triangles inside the revamped circle.

"Now what?" asked George. "Do we close our eyes again and think about Lilith harder?"

"That's exactly what we do," said Fatima. "And no need to get sarky about it. This is important."

The new ring of George, Fatima, Rahim, Maryam, Fabio, and Victoria lay around the inside edge and held hands. "Did we arrange ourselves boy-girl-boy on purpose?" asked George.

Victoria turned her head and looked at Fabio, who was looking back. "George," said Fatima. "You're wearing me out. Which is a good thing, as we need to fall asleep. But I think everyone would be thankful if you stopped talking." Fatima gave George's hand a conciliatory squeeze. The sound of George's mouth opening and shutting was the loudest thing in the room. They closed their eyes.

Fatima was aware of only George's hand in hers.

Rahim must have loosened his grip. The music was too loud, carnival music, a steam organ, a calliope, buzzing bass notes topped by wild runs into piercing upper registers. It was a tune, but so full of accordion-like flourishes that it was hard to name it. Something traditional no doubt, folk, but unfamiliar. She opened her eyes, and the world lurched. A beautiful alabaster horse was right in front of her, its leaps and plunges missing her face by inches. Worse, the ground beneath her feet was moving. Not moving, turning. She and George were on a rotating platform, concentric circles of wheels within wheels.

Fatima could see Victoria and Fabio through a line of horses, each horse transfixed by a striped pole. Behind her, half-obscured by the rise and fall of the lunging horse, stood Rahim and Maryam, holding hands. The canopy above them was painted gold and decorated with circus figures. The music was so loud she could hardly think. Was the carousel speeding up? The carved faces of the horses seemed wild, tongues fallen out of mouths, eyes rolled in pain. It was speeding up! The wind of their passage was starting to howl, a deranged accompaniment to the deafening organ. Vic was shouted something at her she couldn't hear. She saw Fabio hoist Vic onto...what was that? A giraffe? "GEORGE!" she shouted. "WE NEED TO GET ON THE HORSE." He was already moving, a sturdy if not elegant leg thrown over the back, his firm grip tugging her into the lacquered saddle behind him.

She risked a look back despite the swooping and diving of the horse. The motion of all the horses, and not-horses, steeds of a strange menagerie, was more exaggerated than a moment before. Rahim and Maryam had mounted some kind of griffon. There was a swoosh so loud it swamped the music as the roof lifted away. And the ground. Fatima looked down. The mechanism of the carousel was naked beneath them, gears and pipes exposed like a tattooed man without his shirt. Were they flying? "GEORGE! WHAT'S GOING ON?"

"HANG ON," he screamed back. The carousel platform continued to accelerate, spinning faster and rising higher into a black sky. The horse below them rippled and shook, paint cracking off skin to reveal a live horse underneath. George let go of a disconnected length of pole to grab for the mane with his free hand. His other hand still on hers in a death grip. He pulled her arm across his chest. "THIS ISN'T REAL," he shouted. Vic and Fabio's giraffe grew taller, its neck rising obscenely out of sight into a fog of unlit clouds. Fatima could see Vic clinging with both arms to the mottled spots of the giraffe's neck, Fabio's arms wrapped equally tightly around Vic.

The outer ring of horses, no longer stuck by poles to the deck, scrabbled on the edge of the spinning disk. Their own horse struggled against the buffeting wind, hoofs stumbling on the exposed metal rails. First one, then several, fell over the side. Fatima watched in horror as the fallen horses turned into dots. They shrank so rapidly from sight she could only briefly track light-grey points as they fell. George shouted, "WE NEED TO GET ON THE TIGER." There was a full-size tiger to their left, its claws dug into one of the few remaining wooden sections of the carousel floor. The tiger lifted its head and roared. Its teeth and hot breath seemed real enough. Their horse reared high with panic, exposing them to a burst of wind. They were blasted off the ride. The horse tumbled away. George's hands ripped free from first the mane, then Fatima's. "THE BABY," screamed George. "I LOVE YOU."

She was tumbling in space. George fell further away with each rotation. Fatima was dimly aware of other creatures falling beside her in the night. Was that Vic? A pink scarf streamed behind one like a deranged tassel. Must be Maryam. Something struck her head, and the world went completely black.

IN CONVERSATION WITH OLD MASTERS

Fabio falls out, Vic drives down memory lane, Dan swears more than usual

Fatima awoke on the floor of the studio with a splitting headache. She checked her midriff and felt the correct amount of awkward discomfort. George was next to her but gentlemanly turned away, coughing and dry heaving. Maryam helped a drawn-looking Rahim stand, chalk dust in his hair. The pink hijab she had been wearing was torn to confetti, its fabric a ragged pile of scraps at her feet. Where were Vic and Fabio? The studio door was open. Fatima was sure they had locked it before they began.

"At least you don't have to worry about getting it in your hair." Vic's voice rang out from the corridor.

"Sure, fine," said Fabio, the hallway echoing into the studio. "It's still distressing to vomit all over oneself."

"That t-shirt was a right-off anyway. At least you can wear your jacket." Vic rounded the doorframe. "Hiya."

She gave a shy half-wave.

"Ms. Vic, when I woke up and you were gone, I did not know what to think." Rahim literally vibrated, hanging onto Maryam but oscillating towards Vic. He subsided after a moment, hand firmly in Maryam's. Wise man, thought Fatima.

"We're fine. Fabio got a bit dizzy and spewed." Vic dragged an again shirtless Fabio into the room. "We woke before you did. Thought we'd clean up before we disturbed the sleeping beauties."

Maryam crouched down and made a start of sweeping up the tatters of her headscarf with her fingers. "What happened?" she asked.

"Were you on the carousel?" replied Vic.

"Yes," said Maryam. "We all were. And then it got...strange. We ended up on a horse."

"The whole thing lifted off like a UFO," added Fatima.

"Right," said Maryam. "The horses. We fell off. What happened to you?"

"It was amazing!" said Fabio. He'd rescued his jacket from the tool rack, but a triangle of shiny chest still made its presence felt. "The spiders were mind-blowing."

"What spiders?" asked Fatima.

"The safety net thing," replied Fabio. "You didn't see it?"

"No. We were falling. And then we woke up. Right,

love?" George nodded agreement to Fatima's question, but slowly. He was clearly not himself.

"It was INSANE," continued Fabio. "We were falling, and then we landed in this giant...Vic, how would you describe it?"

"It was a giant spider's web. Like a hammock. It broke our fall."

"Yeah, we'd lost the...I think it was a giraffe. Fatima, Vixen has strong arms."

"Must be all the swimming," said Fatima.

"Right. She held onto that giraffe, and I held onto her in an absolutely howling wind. It was bonkers. But I'm glad she eventually had to let go. The giraffe missed the net, or the web, whatever it was, and...."

"And?" asked Fatima.

"Well, it kind of exploded when it hit the ground. Foul, actually. Its legs shattered and its belly ruptured. I think it was dead before the head bounced."

George turned a new shade of green and clutched his stomach. "We get the picture," said Fatima. "What happened to the two of you?"

Fabio continued, "The web caught us and slowed us down as it stretched. We bounced for a bit, and then, there we were, gentle as could be. It's a good thing I'm afraid of snakes and not spiders. These huge...arachnids crept down the net at us, black and red and venomous looking. Then Vic said–"

"'I'm here to see Mum.'" Victoria put her hand on Fabio's shoulder. "They bundled us into cocoons and took us to her."

"That was also wild," said Fabio. "Couldn't see a thing. We were carried for a while. There was this strong smell of chlorine."

"She gassed us," said Vic. "Tear gas. So we would cry."

"Right. That makes sense." Fabio shrugged. "Stung like mad. But the tears dissolved the cocoon. We were in an art gallery. The walls were amazing. Really good stuff. I think Vermeer, Rembrandt, maybe Titian–"

"We were trussed on a cold marble floor. Mum was on the leather bench of course, in those stupid heels with the red soles."

"She's got great legs," said Fabio.

"Are you really going to compliment a woman who called you a 'creature'?" asked Vic.

"Yeah, fair. That was a low point. I think she said," Fabio tried to mimic a sultry voice, "'Oh, Victoria, what manner of creature are you associating with now?'" He returned to his normal voice. "Then one of the spiders bit me, and I woke up."

Fatima helped George into a semi-standing position, if still bent at the waist. She sent Victoria a demanding look, rubbing his back. "Then what?"

"Then we had a chat. Between the two of us. We sat on the bench and discussed the situation. She seemed to understand. Phillip is coming. And I woke up."

"As easy as that."

As easy as world peace. Vic thought back to the art gallery. Which wasn't an art gallery, but a museum. Vast openings flanked by columns that led to rooms in every direction. Vic wasn't the most read up on Old Masters. If she recognized the paintings, they must be big. And they all looked familiar, almost twee. Did Mum have to have Girl with a Pearl Earring in her personal collection? The floor was cold. Intentionally so. She could fix this.

Vic poked at the still figure of Fabio, still half-cocooned. "That was unfriendly," she said.

"She'll be fine in your world." Lilith leaned an elbow on crossed legs and looked down at Victoria.

"He goes by he in my world."

"Another good reason to stay there and not here," replied Lilith. "Why are you here?"

Vic tore the remaining spider silk off her legs and stood before answering. "Yeah, good question. To help you, I think. Maybe to get help. To talk to my mother like a person. Perhaps get some advice."

"Interesting. Why the urgency? I heard the first call, when you were five."

"And ignored it?"

"I needed to be sure this was important." Lilith reached into a sleek black clutch embossed with an elegant gold L. She removed her black cigarette holder from the red leather interior. A neat flick of her wrist made it obvious that the cigarette holder was longer than the purse it travelled in, even before a lit cigarette appeared at its tip. The trail of smoke formed a cursive L before dissipating. "Do tell."

"I met with Dan," said Vic.

"That loathsome man."

"Agreed. Thing is..."

Lilith raised her chin. "Yes?"

"He's broke. And desperate. He asked me to convince you to send Phillip to meet with him. Tomorrow."

"We've discussed this, Victoria."

"I know." Vic sat on the bench next to her mother. "But I've learned a few things since." Vic held up a preventative hand. "He's definitely going to kill Phillip. That's a given. But only after Phillip gives him some kind of password, a password that I think will unlock a fat bank account."

"I have convinced Phillip not to listen to Dan's summons."

"You're lying."

"Why would I lie? You may be my daughter, but you

have chosen to be a fleeting thing. Fifty, maybe sixty more years at most. I have no need to lie. To you."

"Not to me," said Vic. "You're lying to yourself. Phillip can't stay away. Deep down, you know it too." Lilith started to interrupt but Victoria grabbed her arm. "There's more. Listen to me. Dan is one of them. A ghoul. He eats people. Dad's necklace reacted to him."

"That's my necklace," replied Lilith. "Your father gave that to me."

"And you gave it back."

"Of course. Because it symbolizes the blessings of a marriage." Lilith took a long draw on her cigarette, shaking off Vic's hand with a languid flick. "And he chose for us to be apart." Lilith extinguished the coal of her cigarette with a pinch of ebony fingers. Red lacquered nails shone in the museum light. The cigarette retracted into the holder, which shrank until it fit in her clutch.

Lilith took Victoria's hands in hers. "You're wrong about me. And about Dan. Of course he eats people. We all have, at some point. More energy than animals, more useful. When we are desperate enough. Or when we needed to dispose of someone...inconvenient. Mallory has as well. Your precious, moral Mallory."

"Dispose?" asked Victoria. "Like a dirty nappy?" Vic shook her head. "I'm sorry, what?"

"What?" echoed Lilith. She gave Victoria's hands a

light shake.

Vic clenched her hands into fists, tearing them out of Lilith's grasp. "I'm not wrong about Dan. Or Phillip. Or you, for that matter. I'm going to that house tomorrow. 12 Harrows Close. Phillip is going to be there, and Dan is going to kill him." Vic met Lilith's cool gaze. "Unless you come too. I can't stop Dan on my own. But I bet you can."

"Precisely what did Dan promise you, to get ME to come to HIS party?"

"Ha. If only." Vic shook her head again, slower. "He promised me he'd give me Mal back if I could get Phillip to come. You aren't on the menu. But I don't even have to try, because Phillip is sick of living in dreamland with you, isn't he? I'd rather Mal stay in the bottle than be the piper for Phillip's execution. But I don't get that choice. Wild horses won't keep Phillip away. YOU. You have a choice. Stay close to Phillip, accompany him, and you might be able to save him." Vic shrugged. "There's nothing in it for me. Except fewer people die."

"And if Dan has to die?" asked Lilith, her face impassive.

"Has to?" asked Vic.

"An inartful construction," said Lilith, sighing. "But to be clear, if Dan intends to kill my son, I will kill Dan. Is killing Dan part of your plan?" Lilith leaned her cheek on the back of her hand and looked at Victoria.

"No!" said Vic. "Maybe. I don't know." There was a brief flicker in Lilith's calm face, a change so slight Vic wasn't sure she'd seen anything at all. Was there a twitch of Lilith's cool lips, a flare of her nostrils? "Dan is horrible," Vic continued, "but that doesn't mean he has to die. Phillip tried to kill me and I don't want HIM dead. I mean, I do, somewhat, but...killing? It's not in my nature."

Lilith leaned forward and looked directly into Victoria's eyes. "Oh, my daughter, you have no idea what is and what is not in your nature."

Vic realized she'd been too long staring dumb into space. Her friends' expectant faces were turned towards her like sunflowers. "What time is it?" she asked them.

Fatima looked at her watch while the others dug for their phones. "Half seven. Saturday morning." As if on cue, the first rays of a new day brightened the windows of the studio.

"Oh, twat. I need to go." Vic scanned the somewhat deranged room for her purse.

"I'm not letting you," said Fatima.

"Fatima, I've got no time for fooling around. I need to get to London."

"It's too dangerous to go by yourself," replied Fatima.

Vic spotted her purse on the chair shoved under her desk. She stalked over to it, unmindful of the chalk circle. "Who should I take?" she asked. "Fabio?"

"Hey," said Fabio. He reached to stop her but missed.

"No offense," said Victoria, over her shoulder. "You're...You're a lovely person, and if I get through this, I do want to see you again." Vic rescued her purse from beneath the desk and faced the other five participants. "But I'm not going to be alone. Josh the lawyer is coming. Plus, I'll have my whole family with me. And if I play my cards right, I'll have Mal."

"Who's Mal?" demanded Fabio.

Fatima and Vic both said, "I'll tell you later."

"Ms. Vic," interrupted Rahim. "It sounds like what you are going to do is dangerous."

"Hells, yeah," said Vic, throwing on her jacket. "The last time we had a rendezvous with Dan, George got shot. He would have died if Dan hadn't fixed him. I'm not putting him in that kind of danger again."

Rahim looked puzzled. "I'm not sure I understand," he said.

"Nobody does," replied Vic. "But I'm going to do my best to keep ANYONE from getting killed, especially myself."

Fatima crossed her arms. "I still don't like it."

"For good reason, Fats, which is why you, and

George, and the future heir should stay away." Vic gave Fatima an awkward hug over her crossed arms, kissed Fabio on the cheek, and headed out the door.

"Vic!" shouted George. She turned, one foot in the hallway. "Good luck," he said. "And thanks." Victoria waved and was gone.

"Shit. Shit. Shit." Vic looked at the line of cars on the motorway in front of her. Saturday morning and the M4 was a parking lot. This was going to wreak havoc on the battery range. Times like these is when she needed Mal to take her mind off things.

She'd curse him, she'd resent him, she'd trip over his clothes, although in truth, she thought, he didn't have too many possessions. A lifetime on the move had drilled in him a certain level of minimalism. But he could be charming, quite fun to be around.

She remembered another weekend, a long time ago, lying in bed in Bristol. She had been playing with the grey in the wispy hair on his arms, gently tugging and releasing, when she had asked him, "Why does draining a ghoul take so much out of you?" He'd mumbled something he'd probably hoped would pass for I'm-not-awake-so-don't-make-me-answer. They had opposite reactions after mild recreation. He went right to sleep. She became wide awake. She had yanked a bit harder on his forearm hair. "Isn't that one way you get energy? By stealing it from people?"

"Ouch. What are you on?" he'd asked, or something similar, but she had poked him and not let up. If she recalled correctly, she'd slid her hand down and tugged at some other hair. She remembered being pleased with herself for persisting. The question had been bothering her.

"You've taken energy from me, from the Roman Baths, from a bottle of whiskey, and every time you come out...younger. But when you drained the ghoul that one time, it used up almost everything you had. What happened?"

Mal had turned gingerly in bed, blinking and disentangling her hand from its attachments. "Hysteresis," he'd said.

"Hysteresis?"

"Hysteresis. More precisely, hysteresis losses, like in an electric motor. I'm draining them. They're also trying to drain me. Not all of the energy involved transfers. The effort to reverse the flow is all losses. The harder they try to stay alive, the harder I have to pull against them. And the old ones are very good at staying alive. I end up with less than nothing. It's all losses. Especially for them."

"Which feels like a win for the cosmos."

"Oh, it is, darling. But be gentle. You young people

also take it out of me."

He had an easy sense of when she needed distracting, and when she should be left alone. Could she get that with someone else? Was his charm another thing she could live without? "Think, Vicky", she whispered to herself, the dozing red Audi ahead of her leaving an enormous gap between it and the Mini Cooper in front. "How badly do I want him back?"

Mal would have pointed out that autumn oak, surrounded by a circle of fallen leaves in the far-off field beyond the motorway, its lower branches a rich explosion of colour, its heights already bare, spindly arms reaching for the heavens, pious and naked. If she was in a really foul mood, he would have made some weak joke, that it must have been a male tree, to go so thin on top first.

She had asked him once why he had allowed himself to go bald. He had explained to her that at his age, it took almost as much energy to keep a full head of hair as it did to preserve the whole rest of him. He could be pragmatic, as well as useful. But that conversation was now years ago. Chances are, Fatima's nice-sounding scenario was a pipe dream, as substantial as the mist still clinging to the occasional hedge. Dan was most likely lying. Which meant that Mal was probably never coming back. What was that going to mean? She did have to admit that she enjoyed having full control of the stereo. She put the volume up. If only the traffic in front of her would inch onwards a bit faster. 10:45am. She was going to be late.

It was a surprisingly ordinary housing estate, not much in the way of greenery. Neatly paved brick drives, forecourts and fences, late model estate cars nosed into well-pointed walls. Vic bumped over the drive of a random house opposite number 12. She ditched the van diagonally across a less-weathered patch of brick, probably some homeowner's usual spot, and burst out of it with one arm thrust down the sleeve of her leather jacket. She searched for the lock button on the car remote with the other. He'd said eleven, and here it was almost noon.

The house looked deserted, no lights in the windows. "Dan? Dan!" She slapped an open palm on the white front door. It banged inwards against the far wall. Two heads turned towards her, indistinct in the gloom of a deep-set living room. She couldn't make out features, the glare of a bright sky behind her. The long shape of a leather coat gave one away. She shrugged more properly into her jacket and went inside. "Dan." A ruddy head nodded. The other must be Josh, she thought. No sign of Lilith or Phillip. "And Josh. Why are you sitting in the dark?"

"Waitin' for you, cowpoke," said Dan. "Josh here made tea. He's a bit more friendly when a client's involved." Dan put his hands behind his head and leaned back in the down-market velvet Chesterfield. The sprawl of this legs showed off an extravagant pair of tooled leather boots. "Josh, tea for the lady?"

Josh rose from a matching velvet chair. "And you are?" he asked.

"Victoria. Your email pen friend." Her eyes were still adjusting to the light. Josh could have been any middle-aged man in a suit and tie. She felt like she should have met him in passing on a drop-in to Hugh's office. Either he had aged or her memory failed. And who wears suits on the weekend? Besides Fabio, she corrected herself, although in a more stylish cut, and without the tie. "It's been a drive. I will have some tea."

Dan snorted. "What, bad traffic? Or were you hoping to swoop in AFTER the shootout at the OK Corral? No need to serve the nice lady, Josh." Dan leaned forward, elbows on knees. "Bad luck, Vicky. Varmints haven't showed."

Vic helped herself to the teapot on the low table. Stone cold. "I'm as surprised as you are, Dan. I bet Mum he'd be here. And I didn't mean to be late." Vic looked around the dark living room, crowded with heavy furniture. "What is this place? Any way to heat this up?"

Dan waved vaguely towards the back of the house. "One of my many bolt holes. Should be a microwave in the kitchen. 'Cept I ain't happy, Vic-tor-ee-uh. Ain't happy at all."

"I spoke to her, as you requested. Gave her this address. I held up my end of the bargain. Where's Mal?"

Dan looked away with a long sigh. "As I requested. Well, that's a damn fine thing. But as you can see, you haven't held up your end of the bargain. No young Phillip. And while I do like the way you fill out a pair of jeans, he sure ain't hidin' in your back pocket."

"That's because we've been waiting outside, Daniel," said Lilith. "I wanted to see how you treated my daughter." Vic followed her mother's voice to the front door, cold cup of tea in hand. It never failed to spook Vic how similar Lilith's voice sounded to her own, as if she and her mother were the same age. Kind of. And dressed to match the age. Lilith and Phillip stood in the forecourt in his-and-hers tracksuits.

Victoria always expected something luxe from Lilith. She should be rocking Gucci, or maybe Prada. This wasn't even New Balance. More like H&M, although the red stripes on the trousers did match their Fiat 500. Not much of a getaway car, but it did tuck in nicely on the pavement between the lamppost and the house opposite. She'd blown right past it. Vic gave a half-guilty glance at her badly parked van. They would have watched her arrive. Shite. They'd really come.

"Well saddle my back and call me a horse. I'll be damned." Dan's voice boomed from the lounge. "Come on down, Phil. And Phil's mom as well."

"No thanks, old chum. Why don't you come outside instead?" How long had it been since Vic had heard Phillip's voice? That terrible day in the London theatre. Although it was the faceoff in his house in Westminster that haunted her. Nothing good happens when Phillip is around. Vixen, she thought, how are you going to get out of this one?

– § –

"George, you're an idiot." Fatima squirmed against the safety belt, unable to find a comfortable position for her new shape in the front seat.

"I know. An idiot for taking you there, after we agreed to stay away. Safely away." George swiveled to check his blind spot, hands loose on the oversized steering wheel of the van.

"Not that," said Fatima. "I should have asked her for the address. Feels a bit wrong to hack a friend's email."

George signaled to change lanes, eyes on an M4 thick

with traffic. "I know. But it wasn't much of a hack. Her password was trivial. And leaked in a data breach ages ago. It was more like typing than hacking."

"That's not really what I'm mad about," said Fatima. "Spying on Vix. She'd have happily given me her email password." She looked out at the fields, trees along the motorway splendid with colour.

"What is it then, love?" asked George.

"It's that it took us a while to hunt through the password list from...what was that site?"

"You've been pwned." said George. "Dot com."

"Yeah, we're at least thirty minutes behind her. I think we're going to get there too late."

– § –

Dan didn't budge from the overstuffed couch. "What we have here is a standoff," he said, Dan's normal voice loud enough to carry outside. "I've got our mutual friend Josh, and the security token. You've got the password." Vic watched as Lilith gave her son an appraising look. Phillip said nothing. "I've also got us a laptop locked in and ready to go," added Dan. "All you have to do is type the magic word and make us all rich."

"I need a guarantee," shouted Phillip. "How can I be sure you won't kill me the moment the password goes through?"

"You have got to be kidding me," whispered Vic, stepping outside. She gave her mother a pleading look. Lilith shrugged. Vic's stomach was seized by a cramp so violent, she had to crouch down. Half the tea spilled. Sod it, she thought. Time for something drastic. Ignoring the pain in her midriff, she stood and launched the mug as hard as she could into the wall of the house opposite. It shattered with a satisfying bang. Phillip and Lilith both stared at the white powder mark left by its impact on the brick. The windscreen of their car was streaked with clawed fingers of tea. Pumped on adrenaline, Vic grabbed her mother and brother and dragged them to shelter behind her van.

She let go of Lilith and squeezed her brother's hand. "Dan is going to kill you." Vic scrabbled for the key fob in her jacket. "You can't spark a fart with magic right now. He'll eat you alive." She unlocked the van with the remote and opened the sliding side door. "You need reinforcements. Backup. Help." Vic rounded on her mother. "What have you done?" she asked. "You ready for war?"

Lilith eyed the door of 12 Harrows Close through the windows of the van. No movement. "No, Victoria, I am not ready for war. My plan was to slip away."

Vic unstrapped the scuba tank behind the driver's

seat. It toppled onto the green yoga mat lining the floor of the van with a hollow thud. Vic's clever hand worked the hidden catch. The cylinder hinged open on a neat line, revealing a shotgun in a felt-lined compartment. "Well, I'm ready for one," she said. She took out the shotgun and, one by one, loaded five shells from the line of brass circles pressed into the roof of the open case.

Lilith watched her daughter work the loading action of the shotgun with practiced efficiency. She touched Victoria's arm above the muscle tensed by the weight of the gun. "That won't do any good," she said. "The power Daniel and I have is hardly troubled by such toys."

"Is that right?" asked Vic. "The power you have? Can you take down the Texan when the time comes?"

"No. I have only enough to escape with Phillip. And you, if you wish."

"And you, Phillip?" asked Vic. Phillip was still crouched beside the van.

"What on earth is that?" he asked, pointing at the open half-shell of the scuba cylinder.

"I made it," replied Vic. "My dive shop had an old steel tank. It was too pitted on the inside to hold good pressure. Must have been left to stand with water in it. They gave it to me for a tenner. Makes a good hiding place, seeing as I'm not supposed to carry a gun around with me."

"Not the case, you idiot," said Phillip, standing. "The gun. Are you insane?"

"She is, Phillip," added Lilith. "Quite insane. But one might ask us the same. Dan is waiting for us, in that house, to complete the banking you've been wanting. Victoria is convinced he will kill you the moment the transaction goes through. I'm not certain she's wrong."

The front door of the house, ajar from Victoria's exit, swung wider. Dan's thick shape filled the opening. His voice boomed across the forecourt. "I hear you, son. How's this for a guarantee? More than three hundred years ago, I swore an oath on my Hebrew bible, in front of your mother. Haven't I kept my oath, Lilith? Am I not a man of my word?"

Lilith gave an involuntary nod that turned into a small shake of her head. "He has kept his oath with me," she said. "That doesn't mean he'll keep an oath to anyone else."

Vic took off her leather jacket despite the cool. "At last Mum shows a bit of sense. Phillip, he's scary dangerous. More scary than you." She pushed the shotgun down the sleeve of her jacket and wrapped the rest around to conceal it. "And you fucking terrify me."

Dan stepped into the light. He pulled the thin chain around his neck over his chin and held it up. "This here's a Star of David. I swear by the symbol of my ancestors, all the way back to Abraham, I will not harm Phillip this day." Holding the chain with one hand, he squeezed the six-pointed star emblem with the meat of his other hand. From behind the van, Vic could see the brown skin of the back of Dan's hand go white with effort. Dan opened his hand and held up a bloody palm. "A blood oath, Phillip. By the star's points dug into my palm, I swear on my blood you will receive no harm from me today. Now let's shake and get on with it."

Lilith tugged at the back of Phillip's track suit. "Phillip," she said, "I can't protect you. Dan is too strong. I have only enough power to get us home."

Phillip spun, fury in his eyes. "This is what is wrong with you. I AM HOME." He knocked her hand away. "You might have the wisdom of a thousand years, but you know only what's best for you. Not for me. I'm going to live MY life. Not yours."

Lilith clasped Phillip's quivering hand and brought it to her mouth for a kiss. "I understand. Fare well, my son." Phillip left the shelter of the van and walked to where Dan waited in the doorway.

"Take this in your hand," said Dan, fist upraised. The chain holding the bloody Star of David dangled. "You don't have to bear down too hard on the points. It's sharper than it looks." Phillip grabbed the medallion and squeezed.

Vic felt a cool touch on her shoulder. Her mother. They watched Dan and Phillip put bloody palms together. A puff of oily smoke escaped their clasp.

"It's done, son." Dan held up an unmarked hand. "A blood oath, sealed." Phillip looked at his own palm, also whole. Dan clapped him on the shoulder. "Let's go inside and get on with it."

Lilith's voice was a whisper in Victoria's ear. "Now we learn who has the right of it. And if more of your father will be lost." Phillip followed Dan inside, the picture of a winning manager on his way to the post-match interview. The front door closed behind them.

– § –

"I think we've been 'round this roundabout before," said Fatima.

"Yeah, well, I'm not used to navigating the twee suburbs, now am I?" asked George. He reached for the recentre button on the navigation screen, but managed only to move the map further off their current path. "Highland Way, Highland Mews, Highland Lane, Highland Court, they're all variations on the same bloody theme. The damn GPS can get you close–"

Fatima finished, "–but won't get you there."

"Right." George flashed her a look before returning

his eyes to the duplicative housing estates' gently curved roads and mini-roundabouts. "I always figured Vic to be the city centre type."

"She is, Georgie. This is Dan's adventure."

"Even more so, then. He's usually full-on fancy."

"True. But this is the new down-on-his-luck Dan. Desperate and dangerous." Fatima recentered the map with a steady finger. "I won't be surprised if it's a bedsit in a share house."

"Like for immigrants and old people?" asked George.

"Oh, George. Dan's both, it's true. But prejudice aside, I think alien would be more accurate. Take the next right." She held the shoulder strap as George made the turn and wondered what they were headed into.

– § –

Seeing Phillip walk inside reminded Vic of Kevin. Which shouldn't have been so surprising. Phillip was also an attractive man. They both had that confident stride. Kevin didn't come across as if he was God's gift like Phillip, but they both walked in the way that told anyone watching they knew the world was pleased to have them in it. It was mildly remarkable that Kevin was the one and only truly beautiful boy Victoria had dated. He had been gorgeous. In hindsight, it wasn't so strange that there hadn't been more. Beautiful men can be insecure. Or perhaps so used to the constant beam of attraction towards them, they didn't look beyond what was already coming their way. They were receivers, not seekers.

Vic knew physical attraction didn't discriminate by gender. More than once, she'd caught her girlfriends drooling. Like full on, vacant stare, I don't care he might be an idiot, please buy me one more drink so I can go talk to that gorgeous man, little rainbow of saliva a string in their open mouths, drooling. The seekers tended to be confident, if not so good looking. She got plenty of those. Vic knew she was attractive. Still, she never felt she deserved the attention. Especially since it was for face-and-figure, rather than what ticked inside of it. If they hadn't met sight unseen, she and Kevin probably would have never gone out.

She had been required to prepare a design portfolio for her injection moulding paper at uni, which in her case meant plastic chairs. She'd borrowed the department's digital SLR to photograph them. It was the lucky time of day, almost the golden hour of the afternoon. Truth be told, she'd been out too late the night before, missed the morning lectures and a good bit of the afternoon. She'd decided to make up for it by getting her portfolio done. Which was also a bit of a last-minute thing. Her favorite yellow chair was still hot from the mould. Thankfully, she could position it so that the little dents where the plastic hadn't cooled properly were out of view. She'd had the entire hall to herself.

The Engineering faculty was a converted textile factory. 1950's era single-glazed skylights ran the complete length of the roof. Dust motes suspended in the fading light gave it an angelic atmosphere. Or something else must have inspired her. The department had recently purchased a giant set of SD cards, so she took hundreds of snaps. Even the worst ones were hard to delete. The finished edit came out like an art gallery pamphlet. There was the triangle of bright light that captured the path to heaven taken by whoever had been sitting on her white chair the moment before. Three capsized chairs in front of two still bravely upright so kinetic you could feel the fickle wind, or angry giant, that had blown through the now closed factory doors behind them. And a dozen other choice pics. Vic was more proud of the photographs than the chairs.

She entered them into a photography collection and won special jury recognition. She would have won first prize, but the theme of the competition was 'World Citizens'. There wasn't a citizen in any of her pictures. The first and third prize winners were a kaleidoscopic Benetton travelogue of ethnicity. Kevin's well-framed photos of Black commuters won second. Meditative figures in business casual on the bus, the train, blurred from cutting briskly across a crowded square. They joked afterwards that if he had slipped in a few Asians, he'd have won first. But it started with his liking her photo of a chair.

He was so easy on the eye. She'd tracked his progress through the awards exhibition without even thinking. She noticed him standing in front of one of her prints for a good five minutes. He was smooth about noticing her watching him. When he turned to the next display, he gave the smallest of nods, an enquiring tilt of the head. She agreed from across the room. Which turned into a coffee, which turned into dinner, which turned into another late night. And then three months of very good fun.

Together, they could get into any club without waiting. They were also well matched when it came to the sins of the flesh, pre-marital and otherwise. Which was a significant category, because despite his prodigious ability to party, Kevin was churchy. Every weekend without fail, he was clean-shaven, well-dressed, and out the door in time for Sunday morning service. The third time he asked her to accompany him, she went. She even wore a dress. With sleeves.

It was not what she expected. The church was a

converted house, chairs lining the walls from what would have been the dining room to the lounge. The kitchen counter had been ripped out and a lectern installed as a pulpit. Behind the pastor was a drum kit, portable Hammond organ, and guitars. The main things Vic remembered were the grimacy smiles and the clapped accompaniment to the singing. And so much appreciation. Every other word was praise. She hated it.

Afterwards, they had their first big fight. It felt to Vic like she had stumbled into a code word minefield, a secret compartment full of phrases Kevin kept hidden during the secular week. He didn't want to 'move forward' with someone who wouldn't be his 'partner in faith'. They tried to talk it out for a few weeks, in part because he was so damn fine. But he was a believer, and Vic...wasn't. When it was clear she wouldn't be finding faith, he dropped her like a gun.

Which reminded Vic that she was still holding a real gun. It was getting heavy. She was getting cold, the jacket that should be keeping her warm disguising the functionally menacing shape of the Browning semi-auto. An incoherent shout from inside the house snapped her out of her reverie. It sounded like a bystander seeing someone get hit by a train. Lilith was already moving. They hit the door in stride.

LOSING MY RELIGION

Phillip gets mixed up, Dan gets tangled up, Vic opens up, then blows her top

"That looks like her van. That was her!" Fatima gestured vaguely to the right, in a way guaranteed to be useless as driving directions. "Take the next right."

"It's one way," said George.

"Then the one after. George, I saw her run into that house."

"Which house?" George was already turning. The estate was surrounded by a privacy wall fronted by hedges. Semi-detached houses with courtyards. Under other circumstances, George might have fancied it for a nice place to live. Harrows Close on a blink-and-you've-missed-it signpost. George slewed the big van hard right, not quite making the turn. Two tyres bounced over the pavement. The left front bumper crunched something substantial in the low bushes lining the street, but the van kept moving.

"There!" shouted Fatima. "Go right, Georgie." The

van jounced over a cobbled patch marking the transition from tarmacadam to bricked private drive. Whatever Fatima was oriented on was hidden by the curve of the wall. George's tyres squeaked on the slick stones. A sharp right and George was hard on the brakes, Vic's delivery van half-blocking the entrance to a common forecourt. "Twelve," she said. "The one with the front door gaping."

– § –

Fatima and George's arrival was the second aftershock. Phillip and Josh hale and hearty was the first. Vic and Lilith had burst through the door to find Phillip holding a wireless router in one hand, network cables and leads in the other. Josh cowered against the wall. Dan was seated, a battered laptop sideways at his feet. The fabric of the chair smouldered under Dan's hands.

"Phillip," demanded his mother, "What on earth is going on?"

Phillip's shrug was cut short by the tether of the power cord. "He tried to steal my money."

"Your money?" Dan launched out of his chair, sidestepping the skewed laptop on the floor. "It's OUR money, pardner. I was just keeping it safe for you."

"By shifting it into accounts you control?" asked Phillip. He tossed the unplugged router onto the empty settee. "Look, Mum, here's what happened. Josh over there keyed in the account number. Dan inserted the token. I typed in the password. And then that beast of a laptop popped open a dozen windows, each one running a command to transfer funds to God knows where."

"He's running a mixer," said George, from the entranceway.

"A what?" asked Fatima.

"A mixer, Fatima. Sometimes called a tumbler." George pointed at the network router on the sofa. "You send your cryptocurrency to an exchange. The mixer joins small amounts of your coins with other people's crypto, and then spits back your share into the new account of your choice, but with the audit trail completely fogged."

"I don't get it."

"Blockchain transactions are public. If you know a wallet address, you can trace where all its money went. A mixer combines everyone's wallet balance in a giant cauldron." George meshed his fingers together to illustrate. "If that cauldron drains into hundreds and hundreds of new accounts, you can't track whose money went where." George separated his empty hands. "You can still find the balances, but you've lost the source."

Fatima's mouth made a small O. Dan laughed. "That boy's a keeper," said Dan. He imitated George's outspread hands. "But he's right, mixin' is exactly what I'm doin'. But only to keep us safe." Dan put a comforting hand on Phillip's shoulder. "I get that you're suspicious. But I made an oath. Look, I can prove I keep my promises. Ask your sister what I promised her to get you to come."

Phillip shot Vic a startled look. "What?" asked Phillip. "You're in league with him?"

"Go on, Vicky." Dan gave Phillip a pat. "Tell little brother over here."

Vic adjusted her grip on the shotgun-wrapping jacket. Her voice was level, despite the fire in her eyes. "Dan told me that if I could get you to come, he'd return Mallory to me." She was proud of how composed that came out. "I tried to tell him I wasn't interested. He was..." Vic coughed. "Compelling."

"You got that right," said Dan. "And I am a man of my word." Dan pointed to a worn leather bag by the wall. "Josh, can you hand me my satchel?" The prospect of a simple task calmed Josh considerably. He passed the bag to Dan by the strap. Dan reached under the main flap and removed a fat black cylinder. "It's an old camera lens case. Gotta keep the man safe." Dan tossed the case to Lilith, standing next to Vic.

Lilith caught the case and unzipped it. Holding the cap open, she showed the brass bottle inside to her daughter. Vic glanced at it and nodded. Dan picked up the discarded router. "Now would you please plug this thing back in? We'll get all the money back in a minute, once it's been cleaned. You could have your hacker friend tail the logs if you want."

"Actually, I think me, George, and Fatima are on our way. Phillip can sort this one out by himself. But before we go, Lilith, can you open the bottle for me?"

Dan crossed the distance to Lilith before Vic could blink. He put his hand over the leather cap of the lens case. "Not so fast, pardner."

Lilith zippered the lid closed around Dan's hand. "Not to worry, Daniel. There is no way I am helping that man."

"What are you doing?" asked Vic.

"Well, young lady, it's for your own good," said Dan, releasing the case. "Last time I spoke with him, he was bleedin' like a stuck pig. I had to give some heavy sustenance just to keep him from droppin' straight dead. If you open that thing here, he'll die here for sure."

"You won't help him?" Victoria scanned back and forth between Lilith and Dan.

Dan answered for them both. "Well, your mother was pretty clear. And I'm not exactly burstin' with energy myself. Mal's older than dirt. If I had enough juice to fix him proper, do you think I'd even be dealing with your brother?" Dan shrugged. "Your best bet is a hospital. He asked after you though."

Fatima squeezed in between Lilith and Vic. She extracted the case from Lilith's grasp and tugged gently on Vic's jacket. "Let's go, Vixen. Take the win. Goals away are worth more than goals scored at home." Fatima ushered her friend to the door. Dan already had the laptop back on the coffee table. Phillip bent down to restore the router, track suit extra garish against the middle England lounge furniture.

Vic had thought about this moment a hundred times. She'd spot the bottle in the river, snarled in the remnants of her old backpack in an unexpected corner of the murk and surface triumphant. The first thing she'd do was call Fatima – they'd meet at Casualty. She'd picked out St. Mary's in Paddington. It had the best trauma centre. But here, holding the heavy metal of her shotgun, Mal wrapped in an old camera case, the scenario didn't feel right. "George, take this." She handed George the bundle of her jacket. "Fatima, give me the case. Lilith or Dan will help me, or let Mal die, but either way, I am not letting them off the hook." She unzipped the round lid and removed the brass bottle. Its decorative silver wires echoed threads of scar tissue on her palm. Of the others, only Lilith watched what Victoria was doing. Dan was engrossed in the laptop, Josh on his shoulder. Phillip was watching the winking lights of the router progress from yellow to green.

Vic weighed the bottle in her hands. Was she really going to do this, she wondered? Fuck it. The lid of the bottle came off easily. Inside was only air.

The brass bottle top hit Josh in the forehead. Vic had been aiming for Dan, but swimming had made her throwing motion a bit unpracticed. Josh staggered back, one hand over his face. Vic followed her first throw with the empty bottle. It hit the back of the laptop with a plastic crack, then skipped over Dan's head. His eyes blazed gold.

"Damnation, woman, I was trying to do this the easy way. Steal Phillip's money all legal like, arrange for the accident later. But you had to go on and call my bluff. One." Dan flicked his fingers, a casual dismissal. Lilith, Fatima, Victoria, and George were blasted out of the house by a wall of wind.

Bruised and prone on the pavement outside, Vic was too stunned to groan. "Two" carried in the silence left by the shock of the wind's passing. Dan's grim count was closely followed by a wet choking sound. To her right,

Vic saw Fatima sprawled on top of George, eyes closed. Blood ran down Fatima's forehead in thin, pulsing streaks. She must have clipped her head on the way out. Vic's gaze ran to the door, yawned off its hinges. Her attention was drawn back by movement. Lilith bounced up from their ragged pile with the suppleness of a gymnast and vanished through the gap. The choking sound rattled to a halt. Vic's unwrapped shotgun lay on the ground in front of Fatima. Perhaps that was the cause of Fatima's wound. No time to think about it. Vic grabbed the shotgun and staggered inside.

Dan was pressed against the far wall, enveloped by a roiling black cloud. The blackness was so thick it almost completely obscured the gold light encasing Dan's skin. The cloud was spiders, a continuous stream of spiders flowing from Lilith's mouth. She stood behind the overturned couch, her fury a black river bearing down on Dan with colossal weight. Dan's radiance crisped each spider it touched, yet the cloud replenished faster, blasting away the smoke of thousands of dead arachnids, crushing Dan against the anvil of the masonry wall. Until the wall exploded.

Vic's ears rang from the bang. In the space where Dan had been was fine white dust, lighter than the rough cone at Lilith's feet. The couch got the worst of it, broken bricks and chunks of breeze block gouging the cushions. Lilith lay crumpled behind it, unmoving, her hair white and thin. Vic stumbled to her mother, far enough from the blast to have stayed upright, if still somewhat dazed from Dan's initial ejection.

Lilith's face was ancient and wizened, red lipstick garish against the slack, ashy valleys that had replaced the smooth planes of her cheeks. Her whole body was shrunk, as if her track suit had suddenly been remade three sizes larger. Only a low moan betrayed she wasn't dead. Lilith's eyes opened and locked Vic's with intensity. All the energy in Lilith's body had retreated to this one organ. She made a feeble hand motion to raise up. Vic grabbed her mother's arm and lifted her to her feet, Lilith's body less substantial than the shotgun in Vic's other hand.

They were startled by the overturned chair in the corner righting itself. A rumpled and battered Josh emerged. The patchwork of dust on his elbow, shoes, and cuffs showed the chair had taken most of the blast. He gaped at the hunched figure of Lilith, clinging to Victoria for support. "My God," he said, "Is she alright?"

"She's fine," replied Vic. "Old. But fine. This is how she and Dan look without makeup."

Lilith clutched fiercely at Vic's arm, bony fingers claws on Vic's flesh. Vic followed Lilith's gaze away from

Josh to the huge hole in the side of the house. The dust had mostly settled. A similarly aged version of Dan was silhouetted within the opening. "Oh no you don't," said Vic. She shrugged out of her mother's grip and aimed the shotgun with two hands. Deprived of support, Lilith collapsed again.

Dan lifted his hand. "Josh–"

Whatever Dan meant to say was cut off by the thunder of a shotgun shell. Vic watched Dan blow backward out of the house with a grim smile and some satisfaction at the symmetry. Dan lay on his back in the garden, leather duster pockmarked with pellet-sized holes. His chest glistened with blood.

"What have you done?" asked Josh. "Are you insane?" A faint siren sounded in the far-off distance.

"Perfectly sane, Josh," said Vic. "You watched him kill Phillip, right?"

"I...." Josh coughed. "I don't quite understand what happened to Phillip. Dan was choking him, and then he was gone."

"He's here. I think Mum's lying in his ashes. Although it's hard to tell with all this dust."

"But." Josh shook his head. "You shot....You shot him. I have to help. He needs medical attention."

"Don't go near him, you idiot." Vic pumped the shotgun and pointed it at Josh. "I'll shoot you as well."

"Shoot if you must. My wife would never forgive me if I did nothing." Josh darted through the hole before Vic could decide if she would really pull the trigger. A moan from below distracted her. Lilith. She helped her mother stand again, transferring Lilith's hands to the couch back for support. When she looked up, Josh had been replaced.

"Howdy." An elderly but vigorous Dan stood once more in the opening. Dried blood crusted his front. A sly grin creased his wrinkled face. "Victoria."

"Shut it, Dan. I'm about to shoot you again."

"Oh contraire, Miss Vicky, you're about to help me." Dan withdrew a battered brass bottle from the depths of his coat. Discoloured and dented, and more real. "I still have your lover boy."

Victoria pulled the trigger. The explosion was louder this time, her ears recovered from the previous beatings. The recoil felt the same, that same hard punch into her shoulder. The effect, however, was less profound. A tight cluster of pellets bounced off Dan's chest and fell to the ground. A faint golden glow surrounded Dan's body. It was a pale shadow of the radiance he summoned to fend off Lilith, but effective enough.

"Well, Missy, that shotgun blast was egregious. Sure, your boomstick hurt me good the one time, but only 'cuz I was down and out." Dan shrugged. "Josh. Youth AND vigor. Tasty-like. You'll note I haven't yet killed your lover boy. Still can. If I take off this here bottle top, with your momma out of juice and I won't save him, he'll die for sure. You can put down the gun and fight again another day, or I can put down your boy. What'll it be?"

"Why, Daniel?" Lilith's voice was raw but legible. "Why kill my son?"

"Oh, Lily, don't make me explain it," replied Dan. "I never intended to keep my side of the bargain. I lost religion a long time ago. I was hoping to have Josh as a witness to my bona-fides so I could incorporate a business in the UK again. But, oh well. That's the price you pay for being a Warren Buffett capitalist. I like monopolies, sure things, and not being broke. Which brings me back to y'all helpin' out."

"What are you on about?" asked Vic. She pumped the shotgun slide again.

"I'm 'on about' the fact that your Mother Dearest blew up my laptop before everything cleared. I expect there's still some heavy bread on that hard disk, hundred million, maybe more. And your boy George can help me figure it out. But first we have to find the damn thing, before the cops get here. That's where you come in. I'm feelin' a little peak-ed."

Vic turned to her mother. "Lilith, can't you just kill him?"

"I tried." Lilith's voice was a rasp. "Look at me."

Victoria steadied her aim. Dan smothered a laugh. He held up Mal's bottle. "Help me, little lady, and your old man goes free. Try to kill me and all three of you–"

The trigger action was as smooth, the sound as loud. Dan glowed the same pale gold. Again, no pellet touched him. The difference was Victoria's aim. A hail of shot evaporated the bottle stopper. Dan blinked at the ragged open rim of brass. A lanky figure leaned on him for support.

Mal looked around, free hand pressed hard against his bloody stomach. "Hello, my love," he said. "Knew you'd find me." One arm hanging onto Dan's shoulder, he let go of the wound in his stomach to retrieve the broken bottle. "Thank you, Dan. I believe this was me." Mal wobbled slightly, pain deepening the lines in his face. "And now it's you." Mal rammed the jagged edge of the bottle into the side of Dan's neck. Dan dropped like a stone. Mal fell with him.

YOU WERE NEVER MINE

George ruins another shirt, Vic takes a new direction, things return to the Thames

A series of booms roused George. Dazed, he pushed the heavy weight off his chest by instinct and wiped a sludgy film off his face. He opened his eyes to discover hands covered in blood. Fatima! She lay heaped on her side where he had shoved her, quiet. He crawled over and found a thin curtain of blood flowing from her hairline. Hard way to change your hair colour, he thought, kneeling to remove his jacket and t-shirt. He wiped her face with a never-to-be-worn-again Uriah Heep concert t-shirt.

Fatima gave a strangled "mrphh" from beneath the bloody t-shirt. "Stop. What? What are you doing?" she asked.

"Are you ok?" asked George. "How's the baby?"

"Probably retarded from lack of oxygen. Were you trying to smother me?"

"Stopping the bleeding," replied George. "You've got

a head wound."

"That explains the massive headache. It's like my brain's exploding."

"That's not the only thing exploding," said George. "Look at that door."

Fatima clutched at her belly and tried to sit upright. "Where's Vic?" she asked.

"Not sure. Inside, I think."

"That's where we need to be then. Help me up, Georgie."

"Don't you think you should wait in the van?" asked George. "You're a bit banged up."

"No, George, I don't bloody think I should wait in the fucking van. If Vic's in there, she's probably in trouble." Fatima tried to rise on her own but sat back, dizzy. "Leave me. Go."

"Fine. I'll go have a look." George put his jacket on over his bare chest and went to the broken door. "Keep pressure on it. You're still bleeding."

The inside of the house was carnage, furniture tossed around by a colossal child's hand. Probably Dan's, thought George. Lilith was upright, but looked like her body had been swapped for a wax cadaver. She was propped up by the upturned sofa. Only a faint wobble indicated she was alive. No sign of Phillip, Josh, or Dan.

George tentatively picked up Victoria's abandoned shotgun. The scent of gunfire was strong. Afternoon sun shone in through a huge hole in the wall. Also coming through the wall was a low voice, marked with expletives. Unmistakably that of the shotgun's rightful owner.

Victoria knelt beside Mal on the ground. She cupped his face in her hands. "Fucking hell, Mal, fuck. What did you do?"

"I stabbed him." Mal's voice was low.

"I'll say. Bit crude. Couldn't you take his magic or something?"

"Always needed magic less than Dan," replied Mal.

"You sure as fuck need some now. Fuck, Mal. You killed Dan. And I think I've killed you."

"Shhh. Didn't kill me. Did the right thing." Mal shifted, feeble hands trying to keep pressure on the still fresh wound in his gut. The lines in his face flashed a message Vic could not interpret.

"You're dying," she said. "Mal, I don't have time to get you to a hospital. You need to take a year of my life, like you did before."

"Can't." His voice was a whisper.

"Can't, or won't?" Victoria gently moved his hands away. "Fucking hell, Mal. Do you have any blood left?"

"Won't," he said. "Won't give you that hunger. Dan was right. It's time."

"Shut. The fuck. Up. It's not yet time." Vic put her hands over his against the wound, trying to stop the pulsing flow. "There is so much I need to tell you."

"I know. We love each other. Very fine." Mal's body spasmed under their joined hands. "I've had a good run. Long run." He coughed. "Be good to your mother."

"No, Mal, I won't do that either. Take my life. Take another year."

"Won't be enough. Too damaged. I–"

Victoria's hands sank into a cushion of dust. She curled her hands around it and pounded fists of ash into the ground. "There is so much I need to tell you." But there was no Mal to tell it to.

George watched Victoria knead her hands in the earth of the garden. She hammered the ground, grass and soil mixing with ash and blood, until her hands were gloved in grey muck. In his own hands was the unwelcome bulk of her gun. "Vic?" he asked. No indication from the mourning figure. "Vic?" he asked again. "We need to go."

"George?" Her head didn't turn. Her voice was soft, but he heard her.

"Yeah. Vic, it's George." He cautiously stepped through the wall of the house. "We need to go. Can you hear the sirens?"

"I hear them." Her fists drilled moist craters deeper into the lawn. "He's gone, George."

"Dan?"

"Yeah. Him too." Vic pushed herself out of a crouch with muddy, bloody fists. "Mal, George. Mal's gone."

"What do you mean?" asked George. "The bottle was empty."

"There were two," replied Vic. She reached down and retrieved Mal's murder weapon. "Two bottles." She showed George the broken, jagged remains.

"Ah, shite. Is he..."

"Yeah. Let's go." Vic stacked the damaged bottle on the shelf of the shotgun in George's cradled arms. She stalked into the house. "We should find that laptop. Fatima would want it for her story."

"Uh, yeah. Fatima!" George dropped his awkward parcel and ran past her through the living room.

Vic wiped her grey hands on the fabric of the couch, careful not to tip it onto her mother. Lilith clung to the edge, warily. "I need to leave, but I've got nothing left," she said. "There's nothing for me here."

"You've got me," replied Vic.

"Ha." Lilith's laugh was barely more than breath. "You were never mine."

Vic regarded her mother. "I could be."

"It doesn't matter," said Lilith. "I'll be dead soon. And you'll be in gaol."

"I intend to avoid that. Have you seen Dan's laptop?"

Lilith shook her head, stiff and slow. "I have no feel for these devices." Lilith latched a claw hand into Vic's shoulder. "Devices! Do you have anything else from your father? I might heal. And leave."

"Can't you take from me?"

"Aye. I could." Lilith blinked slowly. "I heard what Mal said." She sighed. "You really did love each other."

"What nonsense are you talking?" asked Vic.

"Dan was right, Victoria. Mal was right. We're done. I'm done."

Vic reached inside the neck of her t-shirt, smearing her front with what muck she hadn't wiped off. She pulled out the kasimala. "What about this?"

Lilith inhaled sharply. "Perhaps. Yes. Give it to me."

"It's supposed to be yours anyway. It's your marriage thing, right?" Vic unfastened the chain and put it around her mother's neck. The gold winked darkly in the failing light.

"It was mine, and I gave it up willingly." Lilith closed her eyes, a skeletal hand pinning the necklace to her chest. "With this," she said, "I can haunt you forever."

"Do it," said Vic. "You're not as scary as you think. Get

away. Get out of here." A rivulet of dull beads bounced on the floor. Lilith was gone.

– § –

"You could have helped, you know." Vic was wearing another of George's t-shirts. They were settled in Fatima and George's lounge, the flaming letters of Knights in Satan's Service disturbing the domesticity. There was no alternative. Fatima's clothes really were too small for her. "It was a real fiasco, trying to find that laptop. Then carrying it, and the gun, to the van."

George rotated the half laptop back and forth on the floor. Jagged wires reached helplessly for a monitor portion irretrievably gone. "I think I can make it work," he said, not looking up. "Hope you got rid of the gun."

"In the Thames," said Vic. "With the broken bottle."

"Oh, Vix," said Fatima. "I'm so sorry."

"It's alright, Fats." Vic looked down. "Well, yeah, it's not alright. But it's done. And he's gone in almost the same way he's been missing for the last two years. I'm kind of used to how it feels, know what I mean?"

"I know, Vixen. But it's not the same. It's OK to not be OK for a minute."

Victoria leaned into her friend. "It'll be more than a minute. Fuck, Fatima, I'm so angry I can't even think."

"That's OK too," said Fatima. "But how did you manage to get out of there? We literally crossed a police car on our way to the Ring Road."

"Oh. That. I went for a swim."

"You what?"

"I thought about talking my way out of it. Couldn't be murder since," Victoria shrugged, "no bodies. But even if we pretended the kitchen explosion was a faulty stove, the finer points of reckless endangerment are not something I care to discuss with the Bill. Especially with my history. How exactly did I end up in someone else's vacation home with a shotgun, a hot laptop, and my background? I decided to go right instead of left.

"Back when I was diving more often, one of my swim mates asked if I would do a dive demo at the local swim club. 'Orcas' or 'Dolphins', something like that. They rented time at the leisure centre right nearby. I had thought things looked familiar when I was driving to Harrows Close. I'd actually been down the next lane. The swim centre only had a few parking spots. They always got full. My friend had given me a tip – drive down St. Leonards and walk across the green. I was trying to spin up a tale in my head as to why I was there when I remembered. The GPS told me St. Leonards connected if I went further down the lane. So, I did.

"There's always a spare swim costume and towel in

the van. Showered off the muck in the changing rooms. Must have looked a fright walking in, but no one dresses up for the pool. Did fifty laps to clear my head. Which put some time between me and the neighbourhood crime canvass. There was a cordon at the turnoff, but a high-cut costume and innocently wet hair got me through."

"It's good you're here." Fatima rubbed pensively at her belly. "But how did you know Mal wasn't in the first bottle? I mean, if Mal had come out, wasn't there a good chance he'd die on the spot?"

"Yeah, it was a bit of a gamble," said Vic. "But a small one. After all, am I not my father's daughter?"

"How so?" asked Fatima.

"Well, I knew there was one oath that Dan was absolutely not going to betray, and that was his burning desire to get rid of anyone, or anything, that could bring back the ghouls. Dan wanted to be the number one only-game-in-town. Dan knew that if Mal were hard-pressed, Mal could steal magic from people as easily as the rest of them. Which meant there was always a threat if Mal was around."

"Sure, right, but what does this have to do with your father?"

"Remember before magic got real, my father was a stage magician? Sleight-of-hand, lock picking, card hides, you know, he taught me fun stuff. I never practiced enough to get as good as he was, but you do get a sense for the weight and feel of common objects. I had been thinking about that bottle for TWO YEARS. What Dan handed to me was off. The heft, the shape, didn't feel right in my hand. And Dan's the biggest no-good rascal you'll ever find."

"Was the biggest," said Fatima.

"Right, because now I have the crown." Vic laughed. "Complete load of bollocks. The bottle felt fine. I knew it was off the moment Lilith showed it to me in that lens case. Wasn't mucky enough. It should have been river-worn. The Thames is disgusting. No way the bottle Dan tried to pass off had spent two years in the mud."

"Queen Victoria, at last." Fatima snorted. "Can we get the queen some tea? Perhaps make up a bed for her ladyship?"

"I'm staying over whether you like it or not. I have to. Bloody EV's going to be charging for at least two hours. But I'd also love to put my feet up. It's been hellish."

They were interrupted by a crunching sound, as if someone had stepped on an ice cream cone. George held a black and gold computer chip in an unusual pair of tweezers. "It's the hard drive," he said. "I can work with this."

"Excellent, my love," said Fatima. "But it's your turn

for takeaway. I'm pregnant and Vic's knackered."

Uninspiring paneer masala was interrupted by Fatima's phone vibrating face up on the dining table. "+65 country code," observed George. "Intriguing." Fatima wiped a random finger clean and touched the speaker icon.

"Fitzy?" A familiar, if somewhat slurred, voice.

"Francis!" Fatima stood from the table. "What are you doing up at this hour? It must be three in the morning."

"Half three, actually. I swore I was only having one drink." Some muffled fumbling as Francis adjusted the phone. "Bloody hell."

"Right. Well. Delighted you've called. To what do we owe the honour?"

"I'm absolutely badgered."

"Yes," replied Fatima. "We can tell."

"No, I mean, yes, I'm drunk. But." A throat-clearing noise. Or a half-choked spew. "Important."

"What is, Frankie?"

"This. Four hundred and seven unread emails. On a Saturday."

"Oh, Frankie, I'm glad you're important," said Fatima. "But you may want to wash your face and get into bed. On your side."

"No, no. Hang on." Faint footsteps and the sound of running water. "Better. Four hundred and seven email alerts. Lonestar Tumblecoin."

"You've got my attention." Fatima was bouncing next to the table.

"I...." A long pause. "When I came to Nomura, I told them there was a big whale we might steal from HSBC. Asked the Bitcoin bros to put a watch on it. They did. Hang on." A loud honk, hopefully into a tissue. "Jus' blew up. Today. Four hundred–"

"And seven transactions. Small and somewhat random ones, I bet."

"Right. How'd you know?"

"Never mind, Frankie. We can talk more in the morning." Fatima shook her head. She went to put off the phone, but stopped. "Do your alerts say how much is left?"

"Uh. Perhaps." More fumbling. "Let me check." A thump as the phone fell to the floor. Frankie continued, more faintly. "About fifty thousand Eth. Not sure what that is in money."

George mouthed 'a lot' at his wife.

"Thanks, Frankie. Get some rest. We'll talk later." Fatima cut the line and wedged herself back into her seat. She looked across the table at Vic and George. "Seems that hard drive might have been worth saving."

– § –

Sunday morning was incongruously blue and the M4 to Bristol mostly free. Fabio had texted, wanting to know if she was all right. She'd text him later. Although, it was a perfect day to take your lover out for a drive in the country. Less perfect day to call a widow. But was there ever a good one? Vic turned down the volume, the ring through the van speakers too loud over the hum of the tyres.

"Hello?" Calm and somewhat brusque, with a hint of public school.

"Mrs. Devilliers?"

"It's Harris. I go by my maiden name. Who's calling?" Definitely public school.

"Ms. Harris, I'm a client of your husband."

"How did you get this number? You should be calling Josh."

"I'd like to," replied Vic, hands tightening on the steering wheel. "Do you know where he is?" Vic nearly stumbled over the words she and Fatima had rehearsed.

"He's in London."

"He's supposed to be. Or rather, I was supposed to meet him in London. Yesterday." Vic paused to gather strength. And unclench her fingers. "He never showed."

"That's not like him." The first hint of something

other than disdain.

"Indeed. Did something come up?"

"I...." Josh's wife trailed off. "No," she said, more firmly. "Not that I know of."

"Ms. Harris. I think you should call the police."

"You WHAT?"

"I've never known him to miss an appointment. I'm worried Josh has been dealing with bad people. Russians. Didn't Hugh Sellen also disappear mysteriously? I would talk to the police, if I were you."

"How dare you smear my husband's name." The phone icon on the van's console vanished. Vic shrugged. Message transmitted.

The rest of the drive home was uneventful. What Mrs. Devilliers, correction, Ms. Harris, did next was her business. Perhaps she'd go to Paris. Like Hugh. As if anyone had believed that.

POLYAMORY

*Vic and Maryam get a bit sandy, Fatima puts down
a horse*

It was time to stain the throne. They'd finished the legs, sanded out the seat, smoothed the twisted fibres they'd carved along the grain to make spindles within the crown of the seat back. Vic wanted to do one more pass with a finer grain of sandpaper, but they both knew this was a delaying tactic. Rahim had earlier placed a screwdriver on top of the unopened pot of stain, one kind of message. He bugged her again as they were winding down.

"What would you have done," he asked, "if my wife hadn't been there?"

"What do you mean, Rahim?" she replied.

"You know, to make the sixth point of the star. Why don't you have any friends?"

"That's a bit harsh. I've got you, you know."

"Yes, Ms. Vic. But my community thinks I am a loser, and I have more friends than you. And a wife. Who would you have called if Maryam hadn't been with me?"

"Oh, I'm sure I could have dug somebody up." She slid her protective goggles to the top of her head and faced him, hands on hips. "I used to have friends."

"What happened to them?"

"Well, Ree, they kept telling me they hated my boyfriends, which I didn't like."

"They hated Mallory?"

"Before him. I had a string of real zeroes who they didn't want to hang out with. So, they stopped hanging out with me. I didn't want to hear it. I think in part because I kind of knew they were right. I picked my loser boyfriends over my friends. By the time Mal came along, I'd run out. And then, pandemic."

"The pandemic is over. It is very important to keep making friends, Ms. Vic. At all ages of life."

"I know, Ree," replied Vic. "How about Fabiolus?"

"Fabio is a very nice person. But he does not want to be only a friend."

He'd had the good grace to stop at that point. Or perhaps it was because Maryam was at the door of the studio. Rahim went to get their car. Maryam lingered, in an obvious way.

"Something on your mind?" asked Vic. "I thought I apologized for ruining your wedding day."

"You did," said Maryam. "And you didn't. It wasn't

ruined. This whole thing has been an unreal adventure."

"How's it going, then?"

"Not sure." Maryam clutched her purse over her midriff. "I've met his parents."

"And?"

"They didn't kill me. So that's plus one in my favour." Maryam gave a tight smile.

"Well, yes," agreed Vic. "Not being killed by the in-laws is an important pre-requisite for a happy married life. So now what?"

"That is the question. I thought we'd get a flat together. His mother wants me to move in with them."

"Some patterns are stronger than others," said Vic.

"I know. I didn't really have a proper plan for this. How do you plan?"

"Me?" Vic laughed. "I don't, much."

"What?" Maryam blinked a few times. "This business? How did you become so successful without a plan?"

"That's easy," replied Vic. "I care about what I do, and I work hard enough at it to figure things out. I did get knocked around a bit. And lucky, if you can say that about a public health emergency. But there wasn't a plan, exactly.

"Before all this, I wasn't in a good place. I kind of knew I needed to change my life. Then I got that chance."

Vic picked up a cordless sander and toyed with changing the grit. "This is what I really wanted to do."

"Seems a bit...." Maryam trailed off.

"A bit what?"

"Careless? Sorry." Maryam blushed. "Um. Radical?"

"Probably a little of both." Vic put the sander down on the workbench. "But it was only me, and a bit of money my dad left me. You, on the other hand, need a plan. Sounds like you've married a family, not just a man."

"Does anyone ever marry only one person?" Maryam didn't wait for a response. "It's not only them. There's you. You, your business. Don't you realize you have my husband's future in your hands?"

"Oh, no. Don't put that on me. The only person who has Rahim's future in their hands – that's you." Vic nodded a goodbye. She lowered her safety goggles and picked up the sander.

Vic glanced up at the high windows of the studio. The view of the stars was spoiled by the competing glow of the streetlamps. She'd gotten nothing done, unable to work after quarreling with Rahim and Maryam. The morning too had been ruined by police interviews. She'd reported her shotgun stolen on Sunday and forced the front door to match the story. Fatima had covered for her, of course, that she'd been visiting friends in London all weekend and come home to a broken-in home. At least she'd be able to fix the door herself. Replacing the shotgun would be some random combination of money and bureaucratic odyssey. But she'd be legal. And hopefully remain unlinked to the fracas at Harrows Close. Still, it had been a hard day in which to concentrate. Now night.

"I miss him," she said. Usually when Victoria called London on the mobile, the line was as clear and quiet as if she and Fatima were standing in the same room. Tonight, there was a low background hum that almost obscured Fatima's soft response.

"I know," said Fatima. "Remember when you first described him to me on the phone?"

"Yeah," replied Vic. "I said he was old, too old, but curiously appealing, like he was going to set some hook in me." Vic was quiet for a moment. "He did, Fats. He set some hooks."

"That's good, Vixen. Can't have all your love affairs be trivial."

"Yeah. I hate him too."

"For many good reasons."

"Sure. But mainly because he's in my head." Vic paced to the other end of the studio, where the throne hunkered under its white tarpaulin. "I can hear his voice, asking all kinds of annoying questions. Like, did I intentionally hire Rahim, instead of a white person, so that people wouldn't always assume the man was the owner when they entered the studio?"

"Woah, Vixen. That's some deep stuff going on in there. But it's not Mal. He's gone."

"Exactly. He's gone, but he's still in my head. And I want him to stay there. I know I'm going to forget him."

"You'll forget the details. But you won't forget the essentials. Your life has been permanently changed. Would you have gotten back on the motorcycle without him? What about your business?"

"Maybe. I'd like to think I had all of this in me without him."

"You did. You do. You definitely do," said Fatima. "But Mal was a spark for you. The flame still burns."

"Yeah, it burns, Fatima." Vic covered her eyes with one hand. "Nights like this I'm not sure what to do."

"You do what he'd have you do. Bawl a little. Not too much. Then get back to work. Mal wasn't exactly a go-getter, but he was full of appreciation for this world. He enjoyed his adventures. Enough to keep after them for hundreds of years. What do you have left? Fifty? I need you to make the most of them. I'm not having my baby's godmother be boring. I'm not boring. Did you see the latest?"

"You mean your 'Red Stallion Runaways' article?" Tracing through Dan's hard drive, George stumbled upon the reason why the house at Harrows Close felt unoccupied. Turns out, Dan still had a thriving online business. Or rather, a copy-paste-repeat set of businesses. Working with an offshore web developer, he'd created a series of real-looking cruise travel websites, complete with reviews and comments. Dan had a mailing list of old age pensioners bought from the dark web. He'd email the first hundred a guaranteed-to-win online lottery offer for a free cruise to Bari, Italy. It was supposedly a promotion to advertise a new cruise line and ship. No catch, no fees, airfare included. The only requirement was to email at least five friends, copy the travel site, that they had won a cruise along the Italian coast, a month of absolutely free travel, and agree in exchange that their likeness could be used in advertising. Those who emailed back would be asked for their home address so that a representative of Red Horse Cruise Lines could photograph the happy winners personally receiving their tickets. Or Red Stallion Cruises. Roan Horse Cruise Adventures. Chestnut Cruises. At any one time, there were at least five different sites up and running.

Of course, the personal representative of Red Horse Cruise Lines was Dan. And also of course, there were no tickets. He'd suck what life remained out of the aged carcasses and squat in their house for the month they were supposedly away. When the month was over, he'd arrange to deliver to the next not-so-lucky winner and move on.

George found templates, domain registration records, and email addresses for more than thirty companies on Dan's laptop. Dan hadn't even bothered to scrub the inboxes. George found emails of Dan representing himself as a caretaker contracted by the cruise line to make sure nothing went wrong during their "trip of a lifetime."

Fatima was able to track down the families of several victims. They all told the same story. "Mum and Dad were super excited. They'd won this amazing holiday. They called us when the ticket agent came to take them to the airport. We haven't heard from them since. We didn't worry about it for the month, since they'd told us the cruise ship wouldn't have WiFi. When they didn't come back, we called the police. The police were deeply uninterested. I mean, everything was kind of ok. The house was fine, the bills were on autopay, it looked like someone had watered the plants. They said it wasn't a crime to extend your holiday and not tell anyone. We thought it was just us."

It was chilling. By the fourth interview, Fatima could

anticipate their story. Who needs cryptocurrency millions when you can prey on old people? George immediately made a tense call to his mother, but apparently Dan only targeted couples. At least fourteen of them, although not all the families would talk to Fatima. Enough did to make it a scandal.

"Yeah, although 'runaways' is..." Vic trailed off. She could almost feel Fatima's headshake over the phone.

"We both know what happened to them," said Fatima, "which is why the police can't find the bodies. Got the National Crime Agency involved, though. Ironic that after all those years as the deprivation and human suffering in Asia correspondent, I get my first award nomination for a story about missing OAPs here in jolly old. The worst part is, they all ask me 'Do you think they're dead?'"

"What do you tell them?" asked Vic.

"I tell them yes. Yes, I think they're dead. Don't you? I thought about being kind, leaving them with a bit of hope. 'Oh, hard to say, perhaps they've got dementia and are wandering lost in Trieste.' But we both know they're dead. I point to Harrows Close, owned by the last known victims, and tell them that the people running this scheme must be some nasty characters. Nasty enough to blow up a house and leave shotgun shells lying around when someone got a whiff of the truth. Which seems to convince them. But it's bloody hard to watch. I guess I'm still on the human suffering beat." Fatima sighed. "I really hope this is it, Vixen. I mean, the story is a good one. I didn't kill anyone. But I'd rather have a less stellar career than to keep making meals out of Dan's droppings. Know what I mean?"

Sure, Victoria knew. Who better? She bade her goodnights to Fatima and stalked the studio. Where was that staining brush? Fatima was right. It was time to finish things. And get another motorcycle.

MISADVENTURE'S LEGACY

Fatima achieves immortality, as the wheel turns

Fatima had never been afraid of the things that go bump in the night. Privately, she had always thought it was less fearlessness than a certain lack of imagination. Which was why she worked in non-fiction, the world of the real. She wasn't naive. She'd seen a lot of things and reported on most of them. There was no cruelty she could think up that hadn't already been carried out, no mortal sin unbested by something worse. It's because of this that she could keep the magazine cover of the girl with her nose cut off on her coffee table, the one that made Vic look away. Fatima had to see, had to observe, to remember. Because if she couldn't look, who would? To Fatima, there was nothing more cruel than an evil gone neglected, unseen. She was fed up with awful acts with no consequence, no vengeance, no restitution.

The Red Stallion victims would trouble her for some time. What she'd seen in Afghanistan would trouble her always. She'd asked George to see if he could manage to transfer the remaining Lonestar Ethereum into some private wallet, use the proceeds to setup a trust. HSBC were too fast. Seems there had been more than one watcher on that particular blockchain ledger. The moment Francis got his alerts, HSBC petitioned the Proceeds of Crime Centre to impound the remaining tokens. Their timing was perfect. The bank caught a price rebound following the latest crypto winter. Jammy bastards broke even on Dan's loans.

George was left with the painstaking work of reconstructing four hundred and seven tumbler transactions. It took three months to consolidate the random collection of coins, tokens, and bank transfers into a useable bank account, which was useful, since it took almost that long to setup the trust. They hired a lawyer, not Sellen and Sellen, to incorporate the Har Kala Rashaa Charitable Trust, for the public benefit, relief and assistance of women of Afghan origin in the United Kingdom who are victims of war, religious oppression or gender-based violence. Not cheap to supply temporary shelter, vocational training, and job placement. Fortunately, the multitude of small transactions turned out to be a tidy sum. Several million pounds of hot money cooled by charitable purpose. It all helped her keep going after Vic's death by misadventure.

Vic had gone with Fabio, to Ibiza. The excitement in her voice when she called had been a welcome change. The whole conversation was burned in Fatima's memory. She'd been on the couch with her feet up, a note pad on her mounded belly. She was idly drawing doodles around the list of names George had found on Dan's laptop when the phone rang. George put it on speaker so she didn't have to get up.

"Hey, Fats!" Victoria was lighthearted. "You know how Lilith said there was nothing for her here?"

"Oh, Vix, you can't take that to heart," said Fatima. "She's an idiot."

"No, she's right. There are other places, full of things. I'm going to go to Spain. With Fabio."

"That's a bit random." asked Fatima. "With Fabio?"

"Well, I owe him. He was my plus-one at Rahim's reception."

"You know Fabio's not really a man," said George.

"George!" Fatima glared at her husband. "As if that's important."

"I didn't mean..." George held up his hands. "Not that way. I meant...like if you wanted to have children."

"That's what you two are for," replied Vic. "I was meant to be a godmother, not a mother. How's that going, anyway?"

"Bloody awful." Fatima groaned, then couldn't help

smiling at her own theatrics. "Supposed to pop any day."

"You don't mind if I miss the big day?" You could almost taste the hope in Vic's voice.

"No, Vixen. George's mum will be there, for the blood and grunts. I'm praying that I don't break George's hand in the squeezing. The hard work comes after. When do you leave?"

"Oh, ace. Thanks, Fats. Tickets are for tomorrow. It's a warm-up festival for the big gig in the summer. Kind of a trial run."

"For the DJ, or the two of you?" asked Fatima. George made a face at her in the background.

"Bit of both. And a holiday. There's a dive shop that's wrapping up for the season, but they've agreed to take out a boat if I bring my dry suit. Course, I'll have to use their tanks."

Which turned out to be the mistake. The shop in Ibiza hadn't labeled the mix properly. The tank Vic borrowed was for decompression, almost pure oxygen. She got down to the wreck of the Don Pedro and started convulsing. The coroner wasn't sure if she died of an embolism or drowning. Either way, she was gone before the dive master got her to the surface. Fabio could hardly explain what happened on the phone.

Fatima was in labour when Fabio reached Gatwick with the body. They named the baby Victoria. That was about it for a legacy. The law said that you can't have a partnership with only one partner. Rahim had to re-incorporate with his wife. Fortunately, the Crown let him keep the trading names. But it wasn't the same. Or rather, it was successful, but for the regular market, as Emir Cabinetry. The bespoke stuff was too demanding without Vic. Rahim grew tired of explaining the name. It was a relief when he and Maryam had a son. Emir, of course. By then, little Victoria was almost two.

During her own messy, grieving, nursing, crying process, Fatima became quite close with Maryam. Vic had left Fatima the house and made her executor of the will. It was some surprise Vix even had a will. Rahim had apparently convinced her to write one during the pandemic, when the business turned the corner. Which meant Fatima was in Bristol a fair bit, sorting through papers and leaking milk into her blouse. Maryam was useful company. Seems she'd been excommunicated from her own family but couldn't quite find a good equation with her new in-laws. Rahim made a cradle. Maryam minded the baby in the studio while Fatima dealt with lawyers and accountants.

George drove back and forth for a while, but soon they decided to shift to Cardiff permanently. It was closer to his mum, had more room. They could see the day not far off when Dot would have to move in with them. Better there, than a bedsit in London. It didn't hurt that the bomb shelter of a mine shaft under the house gave George comfort in his end-of-the-world moments. It was a good house for raising Victorias, in any event.

Nobody blamed Fabio, but it was awkward. Fatima couldn't help keeping a journo's eye on Fabio's career, but raves and muscle sports weren't exactly her thing. Other than asking for the occasional ticket, they didn't keep in touch. There was one article Fatima saw with a photo of Fabio out with a famous model that caused a pang, but in truth she was only a little surprised and sad. The hollow ache inside her was already too big to be made much worse.

Francis came back briefly to see his niece, and their parents. But not often. At least the business of running the trust and raising a child kept her busy enough to avoid being too bleak. It's hard to be depressed when you're needed. She and George settled into a rhythm. As they had hoped, their parenting differences were more stylistic than fundamental. They surrendered the shotgun. They kept the gun case. How could they not?

On days when Fatima was really down, she'd sit in the incredible chair she and Rahim couldn't bear to sell and think of her friend. She'd once asked Victoria how she kept her chin up through the terror of the pandemic, the fruitless dives, the grind of the next order for another boring cabinet, her mother, all of the screwups they'd each encountered, Vic more than Fatima. Vixen had said, "It's only a defeat if you call it defeat. I've decided to call each day a victory. Some mornings, mere survival feels like a win. And we're doing much more than that. Mal taught us that magic was alive in the world, in our lives, in the air off the sea, pooled in untraveled glades, hidden in caves high up in every cliff. Unlike most people, you and I know it's real. It's really there. Wild adventures, Fatima. Wild. So what if we don't live forever? Mal used to tell me forever was overrated. It's today, it's now, it's the next now, it's tomorrow. I love you, Fatima. And you love me. And there is so much left to see. Now, leave me alone. I've got a thriving business to run."

Years later, Vicky Junior almost ready for university, Fatima and George took a remembrance tour of London. 16 Middlesex Lane was now a weed dispensary. They both felt Mal would approve. George reminded her that 'Keep One Rolled' was one of Mal's favourite t-shirts.

Phillip's old house on Curzon Street had been taken over by the government of Costa Rica. They'd made it into a chancery. Fatima and George were turned back by security before they could get near the door, but the photos of the flag came out nicely on their phones.

Harrows Close they didn't visit. Neither one of them had much stomach to seek out that unlucky place. Instead, they took a ride on the London Eye. At the top, George held Fatima's hand. They looked out over the city, across Westminster, its political games rolling on undisturbed. "Are we crazy?" he asked.

"Yeah, a little. At least, I think so."

"Did what we remember really happen?"

"You can read about some of it," she replied. "In the archives. Or ask Lilith."

"Ask Lilith," he repeated. "I'd rather not."

"Yeah, me neither," she said. "Guess I'll have to grow old with you, then. And hope that what we tell Victoria will be truth enough."

ACKNOWLEDGEMENTS

Thank you for reading the conclusion of a Dearth of Magic. All three books benefited hugely from the patience, editing, and grace of my wife, Malathi Velamuri, who gave me the space to finish the tale. I'd like to thank Sathya Ganapathi for another creative cover design, and all my peeps in Chennai, who helped me get started.

ABOUT THE AUTHOR

Matthew Wennersten is based in Washington, DC.
Find out more at http://wennersten.org.

Complete the adventure on Amazon.

Book 1	Book 2
16 Middlesex Lane	14 Curzon Street
Available Now	Available Now

Theaker's

Quarterly Fiction

Issue 46

Winter 2013

Editors
Stephen Theaker
John Greenwood

Cover Artist
Howard Watts

Contributors
Josie Gowler
Gary Budgen
Jessy Randall
Ross Gresham
Jacob Edwards
Stephen Palmer
Douglas J. Ogurek
Charles Wilkinson
Mitchell Edgeworth

ISSN (print): 1746-6083

ISSN (online): 1746-6075

ISBN: 978-0-9537650-8-9

Website: www.theakersquarterly.blogspot.com

Email: theakersquarterlyfiction@gmail.com

Lulu Store: www.lulu.com/silveragebooks

Feedbooks: www.feedbooks.com/userbooks/tag/tqf

Submissions: Submissions are very welcome! See website for guidelines and terms.

Advertising: We welcome ad swaps with small press publishers and other creative types, and we'll run ads for relevant new projects from former contributors.

Sending material for review: We are interested in reviewing almost anything that's fantasy-related. We're more than happy to review from pdfs, but we prefer epub and mobi files. Feel free to send without querying.

Mission statement: The primary goal of *Theaker's Quarterly Fiction* is to keep going.

Published by Silver Age Books (we're using up some old ISBNs!) on 31 December 2013.